Mrs. Job

Mona Gustafson Affinito, Ph.D.

iUniverse, Inc.
New York   Bloomington

Mrs. Job

Copyright © 2009. Mona Gustafson Affinito, Ph.D.

All rights reserved. No part of this book may be used or reproduced by any means, graphic, electronic, or mechanical, including photocopying, recording, taping or by any information storage retrieval system without the written permission of the publisher except in the case of brief quotations embodied in critical articles and reviews.

iUniverse books may be ordered through booksellers or by contacting:

iUniverse
1663 Liberty Drive
Bloomington, IN 47403
www.iuniverse.com
1-800-Authors (1-800-288-4677)

Because of the dynamic nature of the Internet, any Web addresses or links contained in this book may have changed since publication and may no longer be valid. The views expressed in this work are solely those of the author and do not necessarily reflect the views of the publisher, and the publisher hereby disclaims any responsibility for them.

ISBN: 978-1-4401-1581-3 (sc)
ISBN: 978-1-4401-1583-7 (hc)
ISBN: 978-1-4401-1582-0 (e-book)

Library of Congress Control Number: 2009920062
Printed in the United States of America

iUniverse rev. date: 01/27/09

To Jennie and Carl Gustafson, who raised us with dinner-table discussions about the delight of appreciating the English language

and

To Christopher C. Wyland, my hero, as he turns his own trials into victorious personal growth

Contents

Chapter One: The End 1
Chapter Two: The Beginning 7
Chapter Three: The Coupling 20
Chapter Four: The Stirring 33
Chapter Five: The Consummation 45
Chapter Six: Fruitful and Multiplying 60
Chapter Seven: Growth, Change, and Crisis 68
Chapter Eight: At Home with Adah 80
Chapter Nine: The Wisdom of Elders 89
Chapter Ten: Piety and Twilight 100
Chapter Eleven: The Trials 110
Chapter Twelve: The Comforters 122
Chapter Thirteen: The Voices 129
Chapter Fourteen: After the Rejoicing 134
Addendum: The Story of the Story 139
Appendix: Proverbs 31:10–31, "Ode to a Capable Wife" 149

Acknowledgments

Thanks to Professor Brevard Childs, who approved my taking on this project in the first place, and to my sister Thelma Wyland, MFA, who gave me the beautiful journal with instructions to get down to business writing about Mrs. Job (Dara). Thanks as well to Thelma for all the good writing clues. Nancy Simpson Brantley is so appreciated for the help she gave me in her John C. Campbell Folk School course and for her continued follow-up with constant encouragement. Thanks to Pastor Dave Olson, who gave me the opportunity to share the trials part of the story with the women in his Bible study group. Deep appreciation to Liz Drotning Hartwell, who gave her professional opinion and granted permission for its use on the back cover of the book.

And there are the friends who read the manuscript and encouraged me to please get it into book form so they could get copies for their friends, which helped with my eager search for an appropriate title. My eyes fill with tears as I remember my friend Barbara McEwen, the epitome of precision, who should still be here to send me her e-mail messages. Gladys Hanna came close to nagging with love as she gave me the constant encouraging push. My cousin Eunice cried as she recognized my friendship with Hallie in the relationship between Adah and Dara. Lynette Eggers helped keep me on path with her enjoyment of the manuscript. Jim Kane is always ready to bring his own writing skills to bear in cheering me on, abetted by Carol. Maggie Fox has a very special way of making me feel my work may be really good.

The gift of encouragement from friends and group members at Mount Calvary Lutheran Church can't be measured. Susan Kunitz gave me the gift of her time and analysis. Thanks to the Esther Circle and the "Dinner Can Wait" group and JustFaith+, who took time out from hard work on social justice to encourage my exploration of justice as it struck Dara and Job.

The "Bears" are so much more important to me than they will ever know, and special thanks to the ones who read the manuscript. I know I will wake up in the middle of the night sometime soon and remember another important person I forgot to name here. I am blessed with the support of so many exceptional people.

To be appreciated the most is Stu Johnson, the wonderful father of my colleague and friend Jay Johnson. Unfortunately, Stu is no longer with us to enjoy the final product, but so much of it is owed to him. He basically took on the job of research into Job's time and neighborhood. My files are full of photos and descriptions he provided to make real the facts of Mrs. Job's daily existence.

Special thanks go to my best critics: my daughter Lisa and my son Doug. They understand that I want the criticism before the manuscript goes public, so they tell me like it is, with good suggestions for clarity and improvement. I also appreciate Lisa's book group, who read it and gave me useful feedback.

And how I appreciate my granddaughter KJ, who treats me like I'm a real writer, and my grandson Erik just for being the great guy he is. Not to be forgotten is their dad, my son-in-law, who keeps me feeling good with his family photos and e-mails.

Chapter One: The End

I will never be Dara again. Only Job remained who had the privilege to address me by my first name, honoring the wisdom which it signifies. Dara lives no more.

It has been three days since I saw Job for the last time and touched him, his cold, stiffened, lifeless body invading mine through my ministering fingers. I am enveloped by the mingled odors of the precious oils with which we anointed him—the sweet smell of lilies of the field, the tenderness of Spikenard, the death message of myrrh, the tangy odor of cedar, and the acrid truth of my own body's anguish. I am shrouded by the vision of his linen-wrapped body on the cold burial slab.

I want to remember my Job alive, but only his mute, icy heaviness touches my recollection. The magnificence of the massive tomb which once reflected and magnified the sun cannot now conceal the truth of his death. We had thought it beautiful with its immense blocks of pale yellow sandstone, several stories high, fronted by engraved copper pillars embossed with gold and silver. Now I see piles of bitter sand, attempts to make something beautiful out of that which is only rotting flesh.

If I could wrap myself around his warmth one more time. But he is locked away behind the heavy bronze gate fronting the tomb. And he is cold. Even the yellow, jasmine, rose, and royal purple blooms around the tomb scald my eyes with their mockery. I will never see or feel him again. Those pungent, costly oils assault my nostrils with rancid decay. Did we really believe they could sweeten the putrefaction of death? The once magnificent tomb signifies nothing. My life signifies nothing.

For the past three days, I have been attended by my children. This morning, Jemimah awakened me—Jemimah,[1] the oldest of my three surviving daughters.

How beautiful she is, with her light olive skin and dark eyes, so lovely she never has to enhance her appearance with malachite and red ochre. How proud Job is of her beauty, of the beauty of all three of his daughters.

Filled with joy, I reach for Job to share this moment and find only emptiness beside me. Then I remember why she is here. Job is dead. I collapse onto my couch, yielding in weakness to the distended barrenness of my own ghostly core.

I hear Jemimah as if from a great distance. "Mother, you must get up and prepare yourself to sit with those who are here to grieve with you."

I am hardly aware of dressing or being dressed. I let my daughters draw me into my royal purple robes, enhanced only by the long flowing sleeves, signifying my position as Job's wife. I eat because Jemimah and her sisters insist that I must. The wheat bread might as well be the barley loaf of the poor, since to my taste, it is only dried clay.

Then my children's presence bears me like a mindless, obediently resisting child from our personal quarters to return for another day to the audience hall to sit in mourning.

Our gilded great hall is no longer beautiful for me, but a huge cavern reflecting the bleak hollow of my own emptiness. The purple that once signified our royalty is now muddy gray to my eyes, and the shining gold is nothing but brown rust. I see the inlays of turquoise and cornelian in the floor. Where is their luster now? The purple hangings interspersed about the hall sag in grief. There are the gold statues signifying Job's royal status directing my eyes to his empty throne to suffer anew the pangs of discovery that he is absent. There are the carved bas-reliefs honoring the memories of our first family of ten children. My heart constricts with an old agony. Had I really been able to view those memorials without pain? I look around and see all these embellishments melt away like mud into colorless palls of mourning.

So many have come here to be with us in our grief, some out of love for Job and me and our family, many out of duty to Job's position, several paid to sing dirges in honor of the king. Finding no solace, I sink deeper into my own despair.

None of these who are here can truly share in my grief. They will return to their own homes, resuming their own activities, leaving me alone to mourn the death of Job, the death of my life's purpose, the death of Dara. Even my children and my grandchildren will be leaving. Jemimah and her sisters and brothers are so solicitous of me, but they must depart soon. They have their own families to care for. I remember how it is to mourn with friends and relatives, then to return home to resume one's normal life. That will not happen for me. I can see only nothingness ahead.

Some here have known me long enough to remember the trials Job and I endured years ago, but that pain, returning so agonizingly for me now, is only a distant memory for them.

Strange how this present anguish sweeps the past in with it. Then I wanted to scream and moan, but I could not. I had to bury that unspeakable pain; I was too busy. So much depended on me to see that the dead were buried, the living fed, and all were comforted. There was responsibility then, and even hope. All was lost, but my Job was still alive. And, indeed, Job's God—our God—kept his promises. But life cannot last forever. Now I am not fighting the torment. I am numb. Our story—my story—is over. I am the past. I am gone.

I cannot give in to this despair. I must summon the will to meet my new responsibilities. It will be different now. It is too soon even to know who will take Job's place as king. It will probably be our eldest son, but the Council of Elders will make the final decision. I do not even want to think about that. Now that Job is dead, I will have no position as a leader of the kingdom.

I do not want to go on without Job. I want to give up. Maybe I would like to die. It has been a very long road.

Suddenly, I am aware of the constant hum of coming and going and the wailing of the official mourners. A wave of movement is spreading through the room. Jemimah is whispering to me.

"Mother, there is an old servant woman approaching—boldly, as if we should know her, as if she has a right to come at us like this."

At first, I gaze empty-eyed at this woman in brown nomad linen. Then, gray coils of hair springing defiantly out from under her head scarf stab deep into my body, unlatching a long-protected memory. It is Adah, on her knees now.

"Dara," she says. Then, as in a ritual, "Forgive me; forgive me; forgive me."

I stop breathing, and then the tears erupt as I plummet into the past. The crowds around me become the hustle and bustle of our tribe. My childhood home becomes the only reality for me now. The tears I could not shed for Job become a sobbing, gasping wailing as I run in memory to my mother, who is sitting with one of my aunts cross-legged at the hand mill in our tent, crushing the barley grain into flour.

"Adah pulled the hair off my doll's head."

I am a little girl again, heartsick that the beautiful lengths of yarn strung with quartz beads have been ripped off my doll's pottery head. Even worse, Adah stands behind me, trying too late to stop me from telling what she did. I want my mother to scold her, maybe even give me permission to pull the strands of beads out of Adah's doll. Of course, she does not.

"Dar', you know Adah is your best friend. You two will find a way to restore good feelings."

I do not want to. I want to hate her forever, so I make her go away to her own tent. I search for the pink, blue, and violet hair beads until I find them all.

"Here, Dar', give them to me. I'll string them on new lengths of yarn for you and boil you some hide glue so you can reattach them to your doll's head."

I give the beads to my mother, but I am still not calm. I pick up the broom, agitated but still comforted a bit by its many colors of broomcorn tied together with stiff flax rope. I bend over to sweep the dirt floor of the tent. I have already done it once this morning, but I need to do something angry. It is hard work, and I can complain to myself that Adah is making my life miserable as I swish it against the floor. Even that angry satisfaction is limited as my mother scolds.

"Be careful. You are stirring up too much dust. It will get into the barley that we are grinding."

What shall I do? I want to be with Adah. I miss her so much it hurts my insides. But I am mad at her. I cannot pretend she has done nothing wrong. I want to play with Adah. But I want to stay mad at her.

So how is it that I find myself outside again, pulling my blue head covering up for protection from the sun and calling to her to come and play? I am not surprised that she is nearby, waiting to be with me.

Her hair causes me to smile. Like the desert driven into waves by the bright midday sun, it surges wildly about her sandy complexion with its iron-red highlights. I do not like to confess it, but I am jealous of those curls and her skin that sparkles with excitement. At the same time, her calm, olive eyes tell the real story of her constancy.

So different am I, with my long, thick, black hair rising and falling under its own weight, and my deceptively calm, bronze skin belying what my mother describes as the penetrating blackness of my eyes. I even wish I were as tall as Adah, who outstrips me by a half a head.

Maybe it is that oppositeness that draws us together. Whatever it may be, as usual, we find our way back to each other. At first, we approach sideways, each waiting for the other to say she is sorry.

Then at the same time, without even speaking our intentions, we run to pick some carob. All is calm again as we suck its sweetness.

We were best friends. Out of all the children in our camp, she was the special one. We played; we fought; we made up and fought again. We daydreamed; we made believe we were grown up. We pretended we were brides; we imagined we were mothers. We tried rouging our faces and enhancing our eyes with powdered malachite and red ochre when our sisters let us beg some from them, and when we could not have the real thing, we pretended to make some with sand and oil. We played with each other's hair, making hers spring back when I pulled on it and mine fall into and out of waves when it was touched. We held each other when we were scared. We got into trouble together, like the time we offered Astarte, our household goddess, a sacrifice of a little sheep that we had formed out of mud.

"How dare you treat Astarte that way," my mother irately reprimanded as she gently cleaned off the goddess and kissed her devotionally. "And besides, you've made a mess. Now you clean it up."

That was not the first time, nor the last, that together Adah and I angered and, I suppose, hurt, our mothers.

Adah and I imagined all kinds of things together, but we never made believe we were old. Yet here we are now, two old ladies, as if we had never been apart, yet separated forever. My memory is bringing color back to me, the reds, yellows, and blues of the rug on our dirt floor, and the mingled oranges and greens in the material waiting for my mother to return to the loom. Adah's coming has released my anguish and restored me to life at the same time. I want to forgive her. I want to fall on my knees and hug her. I do not know. Maybe I have. It is all a blur.

Chapter Two: The Beginning

Adah helped me attach the new strings of beads to my doll's head.

"Let us come back after the glue dries and oil our dolls. We can pretend the water jar is filled with oil."

Oiling ourselves protected us from lice and the drying heat of the sun, so of course we had to do the same for our dolls.

"We should not use that water, Dara. We will get in trouble."

"We can use just a little bit. No one will ever notice."

The blue ceramic jug held the water that was caught and saved when the family poured it over our hands before eating. It would be used later to boil the ingredients to dye the materials for my family's weaving. Little as we were, we knew that water was so precious it could cause wars. Everyone knew the stories of nomads being attacked by other tribes trying to drive them away from their wells.

Adah and I had been very little the first time we knew that there were bad people out there who might hurt us. Adah noticed it first, the way our camp suddenly seemed to crackle.

"Dar', look! Who are those strange men riding into camp? Look at those golden camels!"

My eyes snapped at the sight of their bright red, orange, blue, and green fabric coverings. "Look at all the donkeys they are leading. Look at all the boxes and bags they are carrying. What do you suppose is in them?"

It is not true that we had never seen such colorful camels and heavily laden donkeys before. But this time there were so many at once, and so unexpected.

We had just put our dolls to nap and were tucking our unbleached linen robes up under our knees and into our waistbands so we could play Crown the King with the boys. They had traced a circle in the ground and were about to take turns throwing a die to determine how many steps they could take around it. The first one to make it back to the beginning was the king.

"Let us play with you. We want to have fun too. Do you think we cannot throw the die? Just let us show you."

"Go away. Go play with your dolls or something. Leave us alone. Can you not see that we are playing Crown the King?"

We were too young to realize that girls could not be kings. Truly, I do not know that I ever really admitted that.

And then they laughed, winking at each other and pointing fingers toward us.

"Do not laugh at us. You will be sorry if you do," I hollered as I felt my arms get tight and hard and my fingers curl in stiff on themselves, making my palms hurt in a good kind of way.

Would it not be fun to jump into the middle of all of them and just keep swinging around until I had knocked them all down?

I might have followed through on my thoughts, even though I was almost crying at the same time. Adah looked like she was feeling the same way. We should probably have learned that we would not be allowed to play with the boys, and I guess we would have lost the fight if the boys hit back. They would probably not have done that though, because being two or three years older than we, they already knew that boys were supposed to protect girls.

Anyway, about the strangers. There were lots of people in our settlement, so the hustle and bustle began to attack our ears like a fight between tall squeals and squat rumbles when the men rode in. The boys who had been playing all stood at attention, as if they were heroes who were going to protect us. The first thing I did was rush to take my doll up from her nap. I grabbed Adah's hand, and we stood there a bit, trying to decide whether to stay with the boys or run home to our mothers for protection. We were scared and excited all at the same time. Then we both ran to Adah's tent. I grabbed her mother's right leg and Adah grabbed the left. But her mother was very calm.

"Do not worry. These men are not Chaldeans. They have probably taken a sojourn off the King's Highway to find rest from their travels. It might even be fun for you to enjoy their visit."

I looked sideways at Adah. She seemed calmer.

I guess if Adah is not afraid, then neither should I be.

Adah and I reached for each other's hands at the same time. Somehow, we felt safer that way.

Then things began to happen so fast that we had no time to wonder if we were still afraid. At first, all the grown-ups gathered around the visitors, talking so much we could not even pick out what they were saying. Then the women broke away, rushing to and fro from their tents, creating waves of color in their bright head scarves donned in honor of the guests, carrying out their best blue, and sometimes pink, ceramic drinking jars filled with water to offer the newcomers. First, the men splashed water on their faces and poured some over their hands before they drank until their thirst was gone, using their right hands as cups. Then beer was offered in a large pottery ladle which the men passed around from one to the other.

Our camp felt like a sudden desert storm as the women began bustling about a common fire pit, preparing a huge pot, bigger than what we used just for our own family. The red, orange, and blue flames sent up ripples of heat as they attacked the potage vessel from below. Everyone, it seemed, was adding lentils and vegetables to the stew from above. Somehow, a few people even came up with the flesh and bones of freshly killed birds. By this time, Adah and I were getting very excited. And then began to appear plates of yellow cheese, fresh golden figs and dried brown ones, purple grapes, black raisins, and red pomegranates, some opened to reveal their crimson berries. There were carob beans to suck on as sweet treats, and almonds and pistachio nuts. Honey and grape juice boiled down to syrup were even provided to spread on bread. We had never seen so much wonderful food at one time. It certainly did not look like we were a poor tribe.

In the meantime, the men of our tribe sat themselves crosslegged in a huge circle with the visitors, exchanging stories and news. Adah and I stayed close around them, listening to what they were saying, until our mothers came and took us away.

"That is men's business," they told us.

We moved a little bit, just far enough to whisper to each other without being heard.

"Adah," I was shaking all over now. "They said some people were attacked and killed."

"I know; they had to run away from their camp, away from their well."

"And they said their animals were forced to run away, and some were even killed."

Adah and I were both feeling like our bodies were out of our control, so of course we were getting annoyed with each other.

"I heard it too. Do you think my ears do not work? You are not the only one who listened to them."

I guess we would have let our fear lead us into arguing with each other, but just then, my mother came back to us.

"Go fetch the tray of cheese that I prepared to bring to our guests. Then see if you can help some of the other women carry their food."

My mother could see that I was frightened, I guess, and she put me to work. That did help a little, probably my first lesson in the importance of doing something useful when you are upset.

Mrs. Job

Adah and I ran back and forth, delivering food to the group of men.

When it came time to eat, the guests went first, dipping into the potage with pieces of the flat bread that appeared, like all the other food, out of the nearby tents. All that food and all the special activities helped me forget my terror; I was shuddering with excitement. I had no idea then how much more there would be for the three days the visitors would stay.

On the second day of the visit, they slaughtered a sheep. I knew that was a very special thing to do, but my stomach lurched and cramped when I saw the fresh red blood spurting from the animal. The warm sickly sweet smell of the gore made my throat squeeze and squirm, so I had to hold myself tight to keep everything inside me. It was not at all like seeing the jars of blood stored quietly along with the containers of urine used for the process of dying fabrics. I did not like the swarms of flies that gathered around the carcass, either. I began to itch all over. But I did calm down and enjoy it when I was given a piece of the roasted meat. That was a special treat, because often there was not enough left over for the children after the men and then the women had feasted.

I was filled with fear again when the strangers slept in our tent the first night, right on the rug in the sleeping corner of our tent where our whole family usually slept. This night, I slept with my mother and a couple of my aunts in the women's tent, not in the usual close protection of my father and older brothers. I kept waking up, partly because I was so excited, partly because I could not help thinking someone might try to kill us. I had taken Astarte to bed with me to protect me; though I was a little afraid my parents would not like it if they found out. But I was comforted by her huge breasts and round belly. I knew I had a mother watching over me, stronger than my mother and Adah's mother and all the mothers of the camp put together.

When I woke in the morning, everything was safely calm and pretty much as usual, except that my father did not go out to tend the animals, but stayed instead to be with the guests. Everyone started the day the same way, with bread with something folded inside, like olives, cheese, or dried fruit. And there was lots of it, what with all that was left over from the feast of the day before. My brothers, who were going out to put in their time tending the herds, took some to eat on the way, and the other men from the tribe who joined my father had their share too. The men squatted in a circle on our bright red, orange, and blue rug, eating and continuing their conversations.

The women in my family, dressed in their more special blue sashes and head coverings, did their best to maintain their daily activities. It was a little hard sweeping around the men, but the tent had to be kept clean. Then my mother and one of her sisters began to crush the grain into flour with the hand mill. We usually ate barley bread, but today they prepared the more precious wheat. My mother mixed the milled flour with water and put some of the previous day's dough into a portion of it and let it stand by the heat of the fire until it rose. The rest she just spread out on a dish over the fire, letting it come out flat. That is how she got the thin slices we used to scoop the evening meal out of the common pot.

But you can be sure the women were not just doing their chores. They were also working close enough to the men to hear what they were saying. I did not go looking for Adah that morning either. Listening to the conversation seemed much more interesting. They talked about people transporting copper from the mines and merchants coming by with fine oils and pottery. They seemed to think that was good news.

I did not understand all of it, but I knew I could ask my father later to explain it to me. Not all the fathers were like mine, but he really did make sure he taught us all he could, both his sons and his daughters. Of course, my mother was our most important teacher, because she was the one we were with more often. Even my brothers, when they were very little, spent a lot of time with my mother, doing things like sweeping the floor. But I think maybe I was kind of special to my father. I was the youngest daughter. He was always willing to pull me into his lap when he was sitting. In fact, sometimes I think he squatted down just so he could hold me.

The excitement of the strangers' visit did wear off. Three days is a long time to remain close to the men, even though the feasting was a delight. On the other hand, I did not want to go too far away. I did not want to miss anything, and, to tell the truth, I was still a little fearful. So I stayed with the women and worked at teasing and stripping fleece, removing burrs and dirt and separating it into fibers to prepare it for washing, dyeing, and spinning. Carding wool was really a hard job, and even my brothers were expected to do it before they were old enough to go out to work with the men. It was a task that didn't require much attention or thinking once it had become routine with practice, so for now, it was perfect for listening.

My mother busied herself with spinning wool, twisting it into a kind of string and winding it onto a stick, hovering close to the men while she worked. This time, she was twining different colors together, blue, yellow, and red, in a heavy thickness to be used for weaving decorative and warm hangings. In our family, spinning and weaving were a specialty. We had a reputation for making colorful fabrics, some crafted into loose textures for clothing, others heavier for blankets and hangings, and even denser ones for rugs. My mother and her family were skilled not only in dyeing and weaving, but also in creating yarns and threads of different textures and thicknesses. No two patterns were ever alike, so each product, although it required hard work, was also somewhat fun to create.

Eventually, the time did come when the men were sent on their way with packages of food and a good supply of water. Then I could ask my father to explain why they had stayed with us for so long. That is when I first learned the law of hospitality. It stayed with me even after we were no longer nomads. I suppose the heritage is never completely left behind.

My older brothers and sisters had already been through visits from outsiders, so what my father had to say was not new to them. But I was anxious to relive and understand what had happened. And I knew it was important when he sat down and drew me in to sit in that cozy *V* formed by his crossed legs on the floor.

"Dar', if you remember anything about this visit, I want it to be the importance of hospitality."

"Why? What is hospitality, anyway?"

"Hospitality is the way to look after ourselves. It serves to keep people from attacking us. It keeps things peaceful. When strangers come by, we will offer them water, food, and a place to rest. That is just the way things are."

"But why did they have to sleep right in our tent—right where I usually sleep with all of you? I did not like that. I was frightened."

"We don't hold them at a distance, but rather, we treat them like members of our tribe. That is why they slept in our tent—as one family. We expect the same treatment when we travel about. Our nomadic life is hard, Dara. Knowing we can be assured of food and a place to stay means that we do not have to be afraid of dying of starvation, thirst, and exposure when there are people around who can help. It is really important to promote mutual respect and fair treatment. That, my little one, is what hospitality is all about."

My mother had been nearby, listening, and now she made her way into the conversation. "Besides, Dara, did you not have fun getting to know new people?"

"I guess that is true. I was afraid when they first came, but by the time they left, my fear was gone."

"It is hard," my father said, "to be afraid of people with whom you have shared food, sleeping quarters, and conversation. So, what we actually said to each other is not very important. What matters is that we were together."

"But what if they were bad people?" I was still afraid of the idea of strangers, even if I had become accustomed to the presence of our most recent guests.

"The law of hospitality still applies. We cannot turn someone out to starve or die of exposure. But we do not have to endanger ourselves either. So, we feed the enemy, but in a corner away from us, and give him space to sleep, but not with the family, and one of the men is assigned to keep watch."

That explanation made me feel better, but I was still not totally relieved. I suppose I was too good at finding things to worry about. Still, I was satisfied and ran out to tell Adah what I had learned.

Visits from strangers were not the only excitement at our camp. Every once in a while, the members of the Council of Elders would ride in, swaying in their canopied seats atop the brightly colored blankets protecting their camels' backs from the press of the acacia wood platforms. I liked it when they came to our camp to gather with my father. It was better than when he traveled away to the meetings. I missed him when he was gone, for one thing, but I also liked it when all my uncles came. They were not all really my uncles, but in our tribe, we were all related by membership, even if not through close bloodlines.

I particularly loved Zerah Ben Ruel, though. He let me call him Uncle Ruel, and he paid special attention to me, thereby honoring my father, I think. In fact, he usually brought me some special little gift. One time it was an imported miniature indigo pottery container of aromatic oil having the sweet, fresh scent of the pink rock rose. It pleased almost all my senses with the gentle touch of the oil, the scent, and the thought-picture of the plant itself, so lovely with its tiny pale lilac flower spreading out around its center of orange. The vial did not contain enough to replace the oil we used every morning to comb through our hair and wash our bodies, but it was meant for my doll. He actually brought me two of them.

"Give one to that little girl you play with so much. The one who seems to be your best friend."

Adah jumped up and down when she knew there was one for her doll too.

"That Uncle Ruel must be really rich."

I had to admit I had not noticed; maybe that was because I was accustomed to those special favors. Another time, he brought me an ivory bracelet. The touch of it was so smooth I could taste it, milky and sweet. And the sight was so soft, lightly tinted with pink, that it made my eyes relax. As a matter of fact, I still have it, and it still has the same sensuously calming effect on me.

But it was not only the gifts I loved. Just like my father, he felt like a sturdy tent around me. When he hugged me, I felt warm and safe, partly, I guess, because he was so handsome and big—almost five and a half feet tall. I liked it when he sometimes brought his son Job with him. Not that Job paid any particular attention to me. He was older by about two years. But Adah and I liked looking at his bronze skin, even darker than mine, just barely hiding his developing muscles. He was tall for his age, and nice too. When he was there, he sometimes made the boys let us play their games.

The visits of the Council of Elders were exciting, but not in the same way as those from unexpected strangers. Plans were made ahead of time for a feast, so there was not so much energized hustle and bustle to prepare it. There was not as much curiosity either. Their meetings were pretty important. After all, they did govern all the branches of our tribe spread out over great distances. But there were not many surprises.

One year, they met after most of us had moved into the town for the winter. I liked being in the town, especially when Adah's family and mine occupied the brownish-pink caves near each other, cozy respite from very busy, cold wintry days. When we were living in our tents outside the city, we tended to play mostly outdoor games—when the boys would let us, that is. But when the colder months came, we liked the coziness of playing inside in the embracing dimness. There was such a feeling that these strong rock homes had always been there, waiting for us, and always would be. Even the damp, sweet, biting smell marked a sense of homecoming when we settled in. The older and stronger we got, of course, the less time we had to play.

Not everyone could spend most of their time in the city. Many of the men had to take turns tending the herds. It was not all rest and relaxation for the rest of us either, because that is when we planted our fields, usually in early winter when the rains made it possible for the plough to break the ground. Usually we planted outside the town, but sometimes we were able to purchase land inside the confines of the town. They tell me that as the tribe became wealthier, purchasing became easier, not only because we had more resources with which to bargain for a plot of land, but also because riches buy respect. Townsfolk had looked down on us as outsiders at first, I am told, but later they seemed to think we had more value as people because we had more wealth. Generally, a deal for land was such that it would ultimately be returned to the original families after a prescribed—usually long—period of time, but that made little practical difference.

It was mostly the men who cleared the fields, but we were all involved in the planting and weeding. When I was a little girl, my little brothers and I would be there with my mother and father, helping to drop the seeds or even walking alongside one of them as they pulled the plough. It was not a particularly pleasant job because it was quite cold and wet, and our soggy clothes hung heavy on our bodies, but it had to be done when the rains came.

Millet, lentils, peas, watermelons, and muskmelons were staples. Wheat made the best bread, but it was more particular about the soil it grew in, so we always planted barley as well because it was willing to grow in poorer conditions. We knew we would have enough to eat when we saw the lush greenish-gold fields of barley emerging in the spring rains. But before those days came, we were all out in the fields, hoeing to keep the ground free of weeds.

The really hardest work came in tending the flax, grown for use as lamp wicks and the making of linen fabric. It is only in looking back that I really appreciate the beauty of the fields of aquamarine flowers when they appeared. Now, in my memory, I can almost taste the color. But the fact is, the fields were lovely for a reason that also made it hard for us. The flax were grown very close together to keep them growing straight. That meant hard work for our mothers and us children. It wasn't possible to remove the weeds between the flax in any other way than by squatting down and pulling them out, and that work never ended until time to harvest. Then we still all had to bend and squat to pull up the plants when they were ready. They were not easy to gather. They were not easy to turn into linen either, another job for our mothers.

But before we could harvest the flax, the early spring rains came, swelling the grain, a happy sight and one that meant continued work for all of us. First it was the barley, then the flax, which needed a long dry period to be ready for harvest, and then the wheat. Throughout the season of harvest, there we all were, reaping, threshing, and winnowing.

Wherever mother was, there we were also. That is what mothers did—took care of us while they did their chores. That meant that we worked too at whatever we were big and strong enough to do. As for Adah and me, we liked it when we were permitted to be together with her mother or mine. Then work felt a little more like play. Some of the women were not in the fields, though, staying behind to wet-nurse the babies.

Work never stopped, not even after the grains had been harvested, winnowed, and stored, for the flax had to be prepared for use. Some of the flaxseed that was not left for preparing the next year's crop was stored for medicinal purposes; some was processed to make oil. The flax itself was soaked and then dried, the outer part to be used for lamp wicks and the whiter inner part to be made into thread.

Looking back, I can see how hard we labored, but then it caused no particular thought or observation as we just went about doing our chores. And always in the background there was that mixture of rain on the skin and clothes, or swirling heat in the dry seasons, and the sweet odor of growing things. Remembering now, I sense the sights and sounds more clearly than I experienced them at the time. I think I miss them.

Chapter Three: The Coupling

The fear of attack was always in the back of my mind, ever since the time those visitors came and I learned that there were cruel people who might do awful things to us. But as I approached eight years old, something else happened that upset me just as much—maybe even more, because it seemed so personal. It started when our friend Jarna ran to Adah and me one day, screaming in tears. At first she could say not a word; she was sobbing so hard. Her clothes were so wet with her tears that the linen was clinging to her in beer-colored streaks. We were afraid maybe the attackers were coming, but it turned out to be an attack of a different kind. Finally, through her sobs, she was able to choke out a broken portion at a time:

"My father is ... betrothing me to an old man ... an ugly old man ... at least forty-five ... all wrinkled and dried-up. He ... already has three wives ... but ... they are getting too old ... to have babies, so he wants me ... I begged my father not to do this ... Even my mother did, but ... my family needs the bride price ... He will pay a lot for me ... I have no choice."

It took her a long time to say this because she was sobbing and gulping air so hard in between. But then she could say no more. She just cried and cried and cried. We did too.

This is too terrible. It is as if Jarna is dying.

Adah and I turned empty and died a little inside too. All of us had been looking forward to our betrothals, and as we came closer to the right age, we spent more time imagining what it would be like. But I had never imagined anything so dreadful happening to any of us. I was hurt, sad, scared, and furious. Unfair things made me really angry.

How could her father be so mean? Could Adah's father do such an awful thing? Could my father …? No, of course he would not. Still …

I tried to play as usual with Adah and our other friends for the rest of the day, but I could not calm down inside. I was so upset that I slept hardly at all that night. Even holding Astarte was no help, nor was holding my doll. I just could not get the picture out of my mind of poor Jarna living with those old ladies and having to sleep with that ugly old man.

The next morning, I felt like a thunderstorm inside. I had to do something, anything, because I could not just go on as if this were an ordinary day. What I really wanted to do was pick a fight, but I had no success trying to do that with Adah, because she was feeling the same way I did, and all we could do was make each other more upset. We tried all kinds of things: we ran around in circles; we picked up our dolls and put them down; we tried to pick a fight with the boys, but they just ignored us. Of course, that made us even madder. Why should boys be allowed to treat us as if we were so unimportant? Then we would return to the picture of how our poor friend Jarna would suffer.

When I finally returned to our tent, my mother and a couple of my aunts were weaving. I wanted to help them; I thought maybe that would calm the storm. But there was no more room at the loom. Besides, this was a very intricate piece, and my mother probably thought I was not yet skilled enough.

"Dara, get busy carding some wool."

What does she think I am? Some stupid little kid? Maybe my mother and father really do think I am just something to order around.

Jarna's problem seemed to become more personal. Maybe something awful could really happen to me too. My whole body burst into anger; the more I thought about poor Jarna and the danger I might also be in, the more I fed my fury.

What if I tell my mother what I am upset about, and she acts like it is nothing at all to worry about? Maybe that would mean that she might treat me the same way.

Finally, I got up the courage.

"Mama, Jarna's father has betrothed her to an old man."

I could not hold my body firm. My eyes picked up every detail of my mother's face. Now I knew I was frightened, and even being frightened scared me.

What if she acts like it is nothing to be upset about? What would that mean for me?

She already knew about Jarna, and that made me even angrier and more afraid.

She is acting like this is nothing to feel bad about. Astarte, protect me.

I wanted to run to Astarte's protecting body, but I could not move away from my mother. I had to know …

"Why are you not upset? Does it not anger you that her father can just do that to Jarna? Do you not think it unfair?"

She made me even more upset by telling me, "That is just the way it is, Dara. I do feel very sad for Jarna, but unfair? Her father does have the right. He is the father."

"But my father would not do anything so mean, would he?"

My mother's face turned gentle, and I knew her answer. My body yielded its stress and turned away from the pain in my stomach to the questions in my heart and head.

"Why is Jarna's father like that?"

"Jarna's father has a very large family to take care of. And they are so poor that he has a hard time providing them with everything they need. If he is to be able to care for the rest of the family, he must get the bride price Jarna's betrothed has offered."

Mrs. Job

I could not accept that answer, not with all I had been taught about hospitality and sharing what we had with the rest of the tribe.

"We have enough wealth; why can we not give him some of what we have? Why cannot all our families get together and give him what he needs so he does not have to do that?"

"Because, Dara, that would be an insult to her father. It would be humiliating for him. We would be dishonoring him. We cannot do that to another man in our tribe."

The notion that helping could dishonor and humiliate someone did not make sense to me. I could not accept it. It just was not fair. I was only half listening to my mother's explanation.

"I wish I were a man. They can do whatever they want to. Why should his feelings be more important that Jarna's? And what about her mother, just letting it happen? And you—you do not sound at all upset about it."

"Dara, you must learn that the father is the head of the family. He has final control over everyone else. That is just the way it is. As for Jarna's father, he is a good man, and the husband he has chosen for her is a decent and gentle man as well."

I chose to ignore what she said about Jarna's father; I was too busy reacting to the idea that someone else would have final control over me.

"Does it not anger you that you have to just accept whatever your husband may dish out?"

I was doing what I was so good at—picking a fight when I was upset.

"But I do not have to just accept what my husband decides to do, because my father was good to me when he chose my husband. Your father respects me—and us."

"I do not believe it. I hear him when he is arguing with you."

"Oh, but Dara. That is the point. We do argue. I know some mothers and fathers who do not argue, but I will tell you right now, the wives do not argue because they do not dare. They have to worry about being divorced and sent away or being displaced by a second wife or a concubine. Your father and I argue because he holds me in high regard. Otherwise, he would never listen to what I say, and I would never dare say it."

I had to stop. I did not want to admit that I might be wrong, but I could find no good argument to come back with.

But my mother did not stop there.

"You know, Dar', you could help Jarna if you would stop being so indignant and go talk to her. I know this seems awful, but there are some advantages to being one of several wives. If she does not like lying with her husband, she probably will not have to endure it very often. That duty will be shared with the other women. And when she does get with child, she probably will not have to be with him at all. Besides, there is no reason to believe the other wives will be awful. They just might be very kind and helpful to Jarna, like having several mothers who care about her and about her children when she has them. Her life might even be pretty easy."

That is pretty hard to believe. But perhaps she is right. She usually does tell me the truth. If he is a good and gentle man, and his other wives are kind and generous, then maybe Jarna will have a large new family to love and care for her.

Obviously that possibility had not occurred to me, but now that the seed had been planted, I could hardly wait to spend time with Jarna and tell her what my mother had said. Maybe it would make her feel better.

I found Jarna sitting under one of the few acacia trees on the outskirts of our camp. Maybe "sitting" isn't the right word. She was humped over under the angled branches as if her body were not even hers but just belonged to whatever she happened to be near. It was actually hard talking to her, because she did not move even as I came closer, so I had to bend and twist to fit under the low branches. The position hurt me, but I think she just felt nothing at all. In fact, I think she did not want to feel or think or even hear what I was saying, but I kept on talking.

After a while, though, she noticed how uncomfortable we both were and moved away from the center of the tree so we could fit easily in the shade of the outer branches. She still did not say anything, but I think she was beginning to come back to life. I sat with her for a long time, talking, watching her breathe again and seeing bronze color creep back up her face. By the time we left the tree together, I think she felt a lot better, maybe just because I stayed with her so long, but also perhaps what my mother had said was helpful.

In the days to follow, Jarna was able to play with us again, though I must say she was not as joyful as she had once been.

As for me, the day came when my mother and father gave me wonderful news. Job! I would be betrothed to Job! Uncle Ruel's son Job? Someday, Uncle Ruel would be another father to me. Job! Job was just the right age, too, only two years older than I. I was the happiest girl in the world.

I knew I loved Uncle Ruel. I suppose I should have realized that he was wealthy, too, considering the wonderful gifts he brought me when he came. And I should have known he was an important person, given the special way he was greeted when the Council of Elders met here. All I cared about, though, was that I would be related to him even more closely and that I would eventually be Job's wife.

My father did not have to ask me whether it was acceptable to me, but he did. I hardly listened to him as he made an almost formal speech.

"This contract is important because it protects you. Once you are committed to Job, no one else can marry you by force."

I felt that wonderful big tent of comfort surrounding me that I felt when my father or Uncle Ruel hugged me. I thought of Jarna too. At least she was protected from being married by force to someone who might be violent and cruel.

Thank you, Astarte. You have taken care of me more than I could ever imagine.

My mother explained that they would plan a celebration in honor of this, but, as I already knew, I would not be marrying Job until I began to bleed. All I wanted now was to hug my mother and father, embrace Astarte, and run out to tell Adah.

I did not even bother to throw my shawl over my head to protect from the weather. The warmth was so high inside me that the raindrops felt like sizzling pellets of summer heat. For me, everything everywhere was bright sun as I even imagined high temperature waves rising from the ground, stroking me from the feet up. I must have been casting out bright rays from all over my body so even Adah could tell something wonderful was happening to me.

"Job? The nice one we like to watch when he comes? The one whose father is so rich? Job? The handsome one? The tall one? Thick black hair? Beautiful strong face? Muscles? That Job? The one who lets us play the boys' games? Oh Dar', you are so lucky."

We jumped up and down, both of us laughing—and crying a little too. We went to tell our dolls the good news. Then Adah ran with me to make another visit to Astarte to thank her again for granting me this wonderful thing. I could not stop moving. My heart was pounding too much to stay still. We ran together to find some carob in celebration.

But what about Adah? What will happen to her?

Even as I thought about Adah, she said it. "What will happen to me? Oh please, let's visit Astarte again and ask her to protect me."

It was only a matter of weeks before Adah learned from her father that he had arranged for her betrothal to Narmer. What a relief. Narmer's family always lived close to us, so we knew him. Like Job, he was two years older than we were, and really nice, too. Unlike Job, we saw him all the time, not just when he happened to come to visit.

Adah did not take time to cover her head when she came to tell me, and she did not send out bright rays the way I had, but she was relieved, and so was I. Again we thanked our goddess for taking good care of Adah as well as me.

Narmer's family was not as wealthy or important as Job's, but then, we knew no other family that was. Besides, wealth seemed to be more important to our fathers than it was to us. We did not usually play at being rich, though we did often imagine that we had wonderful jewelry. Of course, we never pretended to be really poor. Actually, until Jarna's experience, I would not have known what that meant. Our tribe in general lived with just enough to eat and protect us from the weather. It is only when we compare ourselves to others who have more that we begin to feel poor.

Both Adah and I were happy and relieved with the choices that had been made for us. Now we could enjoy playing wedding, marriage, and family. It was all the more fun knowing who our husbands would be. Now we could picture our own husbands and children around the potage in the evening.

I think my parents had chosen to begin this process in the winter because my father could be around more often and Uncle Ruel would be freer to travel. The crops had been planted but were not yet ready for hoeing and weeding, committed to future growth, but not yet ripe. A little like me, I guess. And my brothers were in charge of herding the flocks outside the city. Mostly, my father just had to show up to supervise. So this was a good time for the betrothal ceremony.

Looking back, that was almost better than our marriage rite. Job and I were the center of attention, and there was feasting and celebration with the whole family and Adah. Best of all, everything went back to normal when it was done. It was like a wonderful game.

Our betrothal day began when a couple of my married sisters came by early, placing special cheeses and other food near the cooking pot, and then going into the women's quarters with my mother and me and some of our aunts. Not only did they bring special foods, but they came looking special themselves, wearing bleached white linen with their indigo tunics and head scarves.

Being older, they had gone through this process themselves, and while they were getting me ready for the ritual, they bubbled with stories of their own betrothals and marriages.

"Remember when Papa called you my name by mistake?"

"Yes," my sister joked. "Just think. Your poor husband might have been stuck with me."

"And what about Mama at my wedding?" giggled the oldest. "She kept forgetting things she was supposed to do."

"Well, after all," my mother defended herself, "it is a big day in a mother's life when her first daughter gets married. It is not easy to send her off to another woman's home. And besides, it meant I was getting old."

"You? Old?" My sisters all gathered around her with hugs.

"Well, she is certainly older than I am, and she always will be." That was my aunt, my mother's younger sister, joining in the teasing.

I guess in years to come, I will also talk and laugh about my betrothal-day celebration. Right now, though, I just cannot imagine ever being older or happier than I am today.

My body felt very solidly grown-up and yet jittery excited all over.

Except for my wedding day, I would never again have the special kind of attention I had that afternoon. The women helped my mother bathe me in expensive oils smelling sweet of lilies of the field and Spikenard and dressed me in a new ankle-length milky-white linen tunic with a blue silk sash and a deep blue robe over it. The feel of the fabric was especially soft since my mother had prepared the thread with particular care, making it possible to weave it into an unusually fine linen. It was a grown-up, once-in-my-lifetime outfit.

I have to admit I was too energized to stand still. They had to keep telling me to calm down so they could finish the job. The men outside the women's tent must have felt a little happy themselves, just hearing all the laughter.

When I was all dressed, my long, thick black hair was tied back with a silk scarf that matched the sash, and they braided in some beads of pink, blue, and violet.

Look at those beads. They are the same color as the beads in my doll's hair. So many years I have been playing grown-up with Adah, and now I almost am.

When I was ready, I was allowed to leave the women's tent with the stern warning not to get dirty.

Of course, the first thing I did was go to Adah's.

"Oh, Dara. You look so beautiful."

I knew she was happy for me, but maybe she was wondering whether she would ever look so special. As time for the ceremony drew closer, she seemed pretty quiet. Maybe she was just sick of hearing about Job all the time now. But it seemed like there was something else, almost as if she were angry with me for some reason.

"Are you mad at me, Adah?"

"What a stupid thought. Of course I'm not mad at you. You are my best friend. Why would I be angry?"

I was not convinced. There was something wrong. The air had a feeling of a sandstorm brewing, but there was no storm.

I was happy, though, that Adah and her family were to be included in the celebration along with our more immediate relatives, and she was happy to be dressed in her good clothes for it. It would not seem right for special things to happen for me without her there.

When Adah and I got back, the rest of my family had begun to gather. It was so beautiful, seeing them all dressed up, creating a swing and flow of blues, yellows, oranges, blinding white, and calming tans.

Then Uncle Ruel arrived with his whole family, Job and all his brothers and sisters, and Job's mother. I knew Auntie Beta. She was nice enough, and I did love the beautiful jewelry she wore, but I liked it better when I had Uncle Ruel all to myself. Things were a little stiff, and I circled around him first like he was some sort of strange animal. When I did go to him, his hug felt wonderful as usual. Uncle Ruel laughed his really nice laugh and pulled me back for another hug. "This is a very happy day for us, Dar'." And he gave me a very special present. It was a gold chain with a figure of Astarte suspended on it. I loved it and felt especially protected by it. I wore it every day until well into my marriage.

Job was all dressed up too. He was also wearing new linen—a tan loincloth that went down to his knees with a purple tunic over it and a sash of deep brown. Over all that, like me, he was wearing a robe of deep blue. Suddenly I felt very uneasy with him, and he seemed to feel the same way.

Is he content to be betrothed to me? Maybe he does not want to be. Maybe he likes someone else. Maybe his father forced him to do this. Still, he does not look unhappy, just shy. I guess I probably look the same way to him.

Job sent a quick look in my direction. It did not look like the expression of someone who was feeling sorry for himself. I had the feeling that a hug from Job would feel every bit as good as the one from his father, but of course I could not test that out.

When the families were gathered, we got really formal, men in a group in front and the women behind. Then followed a very proper ceremony in which the fathers signed the betrothal agreement. It included a list of the gifts that would be exchanged when we got married. I guess it was the price my father was paying to get Uncle Ruel to accept me for Job, and my father's reward for giving me away. I was thinking good thoughts about the whole thing; it just seemed very good to me that Job and I would eventually be starting off with a large herd of cattle and sheep and even some donkeys and a camel. I was not unhappy either about the gold I would be receiving.

The ritual went on with my father praising Uncle Ruel as the most desirable man one could want for my father-in-law, and, to hear my father say it, Job was a treasured, extremely valuable, unblemished lamb. Uncle Ruel returned the favor with all kinds of praise for my father. You would think he was the King

Almighty. As for me, I might as well be Astarte for the way Uncle Ruel made me sound like a goddess. I was tempted to believe all the nice things that were being said, especially about me.

The rites ended when my father placed his hands on Job's shoulders, saying, "You will be my son-in-law," and Uncle Ruel did the same to me, saying, "You will be the wife of my son Job."

I was very happy at the idea of being really related to Uncle Ruel.

And speaking of Astarte, I kissed her frequently on my gold chain during the ceremony, and I paid a visit to our household Astarte right after the ceremony, along with my sisters and brothers and Adah. I was so grateful to her. I owed her so much gratitude. Together, we brought her a tribute of pomegranates, opened so the beautiful pink seeds showed.

The rest of the day was spent feasting. It was better than when strangers came to stay, because this time, Job and I were honored guests, and I did not have to worry whether there would be a share of the roasted sheep for me. Job and I, though, made a wide circle around each other. We just did not know how to act in this new situation. Neither one of us was very relaxed in our special clothes. It was a lovely cool day, though, the best of the winter season—no rain, but no high heat lapping at our feet either. The blue of the sky bathed us in comfortable warmth, and our acacia trees seemed greener than ever they had been, tinged with white reflection, a firm outline against the mauve sky.

The next morning, we were back almost to normal. Breakfast was a little different because we had some things left over from the celebration of the day before. People had brought dried figs, raisins, and some almond and pistachio nuts from the market, and I especially enjoyed the different cheeses my sisters had provided. The leftover bread was special, too, made from wheat instead of barley. I tried to make my specialness last longer.

"Mama, can I not enjoy being special for another day? Just for this morning, could someone else sweep the tent?"

"The work does not get special, Dara. It does not go away, and neither does the responsibility to do one's share."

My body just would not stay calm enough to bend over and sweep. I needed something larger to do. I guess my mother could tell how I was feeling.

"I can see you are very restless, Dar'. Take the food to the people tending the sheep instead. That will give you a chance to run a bit."

Of course I went to find Adah to go with me. She was still acting a little strange, I thought.

"I cannot go with you. My mother has chores for me to do."

"But Adah, we can do what we always do. I will help you with your tasks after you keep me company on mine."

"No; I just cannot do that."

Again, I asked Adah if she was mad at me for some reason. She said she was not, but it felt to me like she was. For a long time after that, there was that little feeling that something was different.

Chapter Four: The Stirring

The events of our betrothals slipped pretty much into the background as Adah and I went on with the process of growing up. It is true that when we played at marriage it could be more real for us, knowing who our husbands would be, and the same thing was true of seeing ourselves as mothers. But we were also occupied with the pleasures of doing things that we could not do when we were really little.

Adah and I loved the grown-up task of going to the market together. I liked that I had authority in picking out the purchases to bring back to my family, usually imported onions and garlic and occasionally fruit and nuts, but also sometimes pretty pottery for food storage, nicer than what we could make ourselves. We could not buy the jewelry and precious oils we loved looking at, but just looking was fun. Sometimes I got to bring some of our woven cloth or hangings to trade. They usually sold right away, because they were very beautiful and, to tell the truth, I was quite skilled at bargaining. I was allowed to use some of the profits to buy some carob beans for Adah and me to enjoy on the way back to camp.

I also enjoyed the job of drawing water from the well, or taking it from the cistern when we were living in town. That was harder work than going to the market, but it was also a grown-up task that made me feel tall and important. I especially liked it when I got to walk home with one of our more beautiful pottery containers on my head.

In truth, life was quite uneventful—until I was about eleven. Then it began to happen. It was not as if I had not seen it begin for the older girls in the tribe, but then I was only watching. This was really personal. My body shape began to change, and I grew to be almost as tall as my mother. My black hair became even thicker and more grown-up somehow. Something happened to my face as well as my cheekbones became more angular and my lips got fuller and even, I think, redder. I really liked that my skin developed a touch of iron glow in the field of bronze, making it a little more like Adah's. Inside, I began to tickle and weaken in some ways and strengthen in others, some parts of me getting soft and spongy while my spine felt like it was getting firmer.

I had sometimes played with tying up my hair with jewels, but now it seemed to be much more fun and important, as did rouging my face and lips. Instead of carob, I wanted to buy some of the Salt Sea mud that was supposed to make me more beautiful. It took more effort to do my chores, because I wanted just to sit around and feel these strange sensations. But Adah and I also liked being with the other girls at the well, where we could compare each other's transformations. Fortunately, Adah was going through changes at the same time I was. Her hair became even springier, and her sandy skin darkened a bit. Like me, she grew taller, but not by as much, so we were seeing each other eye to eye.

We knew we were going through the awakening that would lead soon to the flow of blood and then marriage. Excited but scared, we wanted to play mother with our dolls and we wanted to put them away. We wanted everyone to look at our specialness, and we wanted to hide. Soon we would be joining the other women once a month away from everyone else. I was afraid mine would not flow at the same time theirs did, and I would have to be isolated alone.

My parents probably noticed the things that were happening to me even before I did, though I confess I tried to hide them even as I wanted to show them off. For some strange reason, it was both embarrassing and a source of pride, neither of which I felt like talking about with anyone but Adah. It was scary, too, because I realized that soon I would be moving away from my parents and brothers and sisters and I would be a wife and mother belonging to another family a full day's journey away.

Of course, I began to pay more attention to Job when he was around. He was probably paying me more notice too. Maybe because I knew that I would become his wife, and maybe because it would have happened anyway, peculiar sensations began to creep in when he was near. Then I would feel a tingle in my belly while the rest of my body went limp. I really wanted just to faint against him and flow into him. He was so handsome with his thick black hair and the pointed beard he was growing. Now he was even taller than he had been when we were betrothed, taller than most of the other boys. I knew I was not allowed, but I wanted to touch him where his muscles glistened and rippled in a very grown-up way. I was coming to love him, I suppose.

The feelings I had for Job were confusing for me, but I wanted to hold them secret to myself. I did not want to admit that I was unsure about anything. My mother was not ignorant, though, and the day came when she sat me down. She did not have to tell me where babies come from. Living in the midst of so many women, and seeing them retreat to the women's tent once a month, and then again when they were ready to give birth, had taught me those facts gradually. But I had not expected these feelings inside me, especially the way I felt about Job. It was actually a relief when she opened up a conversation.

"Dara, come sit by me. Let us talk about your coming marriage. Are you feeling ready for that change in your life? How about Job? Are you happy you will soon be his bride?"

"Oh, Mama," I hesitated, not sure that I really wanted to let her know my secrets. "I feel so funny when I am near him."

"I guess you probably do not know how to talk to him. Maybe it feels strange to know that soon you will be his wife."

"It is more than that." This time, I hesitated for a long time before the words erupted. "I really do feel funny. My body feels funny. I get soft inside, and my belly tingles and tickles, almost as if it needs something to eat. And yet it is not like being hungry for food. I'm hungry somewhere inside, but not like when it is time for the evening meal. Oh, Mama. I hope you know what I mean, because I do not know how to explain it."

Just trying to describe what my body was doing left me feeling weak.

This is awful. I wish I had not started to tell her. I feel like hot red blood is creeping up from my toes into my head. She must be able to tell that I am having sensations I should not be having. I am afraid she will scold me. But it is like something has exploded inside me, and I cannot stop letting it out.

My mother put her arm around me. It felt warm and good as I leaned into her.

"What you are describing to me is just the way you should be feeling now. You have the body of a growing woman."

She makes me feel so proud, and scared. I do not want to grow up so much that she will stop pulling me close to her like this. But I do not want her to think of me as a little girl any more either. Maybe I am still just a little girl, and she is telling me these things only to make me feel better.

"But Mama, I see you with Papa, and it does not look like you feel that way with him."

"Oh Dara, I did feel that way about your father when we were first joined in marriage, but love changes over time. I guess you could say at first it is like feasting on figs and pomegranates and special cheeses, and later it is like enjoying the evening potage. The thrill may not be so great later on, but each day it fills the empty hole that would be hunger if you did not have each other."

I liked the idea of being fed in that way, but I was a little disappointed at the thought that this all-body thrill would someday go away. Even though it frightened me, I liked the feelings I had around Job, and I vowed they would never turn to potage. I kept that thought a secret from my mother, though. It would be too much like criticizing her. But she seemed to know what I was thinking. I guess she would be smart about these things after going through it herself, and with my older sisters too, and all the other women of the tribe who raised their tents near ours.

Still, I do think I am different. No one has ever experienced quite these sensations. I will just keep it to myself now, though.

"Dara, I hope you reap great satisfaction from every stage of love. The thrill is something to be treasured, as will be the unbelievable joy of having your first baby together. But eventually, the love becomes so much deeper. Your father and I are not separate persons anymore. He and I are really part of each other."

Yes, that is what I am feeling. I want to be a part of Job—really a part of him.

"I sacrifice daily to Astarte asking that you will feel that same growth of love with Job. You will see. Eventually his happiness will be yours and his pain will be yours. An attack on his body will be an attack on yours, and whenever he is spared, you will be spared. And he will know you in the same way."

My mother was a very wise woman.

Then came the day when the first pinkish-brown stain appeared. Now the arrangements that had been made were set in motion. It was time to plan our wedding and time for me to really think about how marriage would change my life.

"Oh, Adah. What will it be like? I do not want to be away from you. I want to be married to Job. I want all that, but I do not want anything to change. I do not want to leave my family, and what will I do without you every day?"

We sat together in silence for a long time. We had no answer. We wanted to promise each other that we would always be together in the same way as now, but we knew that could not be. She would be living with Narmer and I would be with Job. She would be having lots of his children, and I would have lots of children with

Job. We would be busy being wives and mothers. There was no way we could see each other every day. It was too much to take in all at one time, so we went about doing our chores, including a long walk to the market, trying to pretend that nothing was changing.

The din and color of the market made it almost impossible to think about ourselves at all. Everywhere there were the temporary shelters thrown up to protect the wares spread out on the ground. Even the shelters were of different colors and textures, depending on the materials of which they were made. Some of wool spun from black sheep, some from brown, and some white. And there were the rugs thrown up on acacia branches cut and fitted to the right size to hold them, some of them almost as beautiful as the things my family made in patterns of bright reds, oranges, blues, and even some yellow. The noise was colorful too, so many voices calling out at once, arguing about the best exchange or urging us to buy. And the smells, the pungent onions, sweet aromatic oils, fresh ripe fruits, and even the rotting smell of products left too long in the heat. The odors were so powerful we could almost see and feel them.

Now we were there with orders from our mothers about what to bring home, but we could imagine the day soon when we would be making the choices for ourselves. We would be in charge. And then, when we started having such thoughts, we would make ourselves forget what was coming and just be little girls again, sent to the market by our mothers. No matter what we did or where we were, it seemed like we were little and grown-up all at the same time.

One day, we put our dolls to bed and remembered a couple of weeks later that they were still sleeping. Playing with them was no longer so much fun. Maybe real life was becoming more interesting? But I was sad. I even apologized to my doll, promising to pay more attention to her. I did not, though. Instead, I tucked her away in a nice bed of colorful broomcorn and wrapped her in a tiny blue-and-green blanket my mother had woven for her when I was still little.

"I will get you out later for my daughters to play with," I promised her. Little did I know that her play life would be limited when our adopted God declared her to be an idol.

How wonderful to think of having the prestige and authority of being a married woman. How awful to leave my family and Adah behind. How scary to be a member of someone else's family and not my own. How incredible to be with Job all the time. How frighteningly exciting the thought of making love with him. How warm to anticipate the kind of "potage love" for Job that my mother described. How awesome to give orders to my servants and children instead of obeying other people's commands all the time. How grown-up.

Do I really want all this?

Job was also busy gathering the wealth he needed to establish our own home. I imagined he was feeling really grown-up about that. I supposed it might be a little scary too. Once he was married, he would be responsible for his own herds, our home, and his family. If Adah and I thought the change would be wonderful and scary, I imagine he would feel the same way about what was happening to him. Being grown-up did have its drawbacks.

Usually, in our tribe, the bridegroom and his family prepared the new home and brought the bride to it on the wedding day as a kind of surprise. I do not think that was so much a desire to do something special for her as it reflected that the husband was in charge and it was his home. Fortunately, Job had learned some important things from his father, so he included me in the plans as he purchased the site for our tent and erected it.

Because of his family's wealth, Job was able to establish a permanent tent inside the town. To care for his flocks, there would be temporary shelters that could be moved, as was our nomadic tradition, from one place to another as weather and water dictated. These would be occupied sometimes by us, but most often by his servants.

It was part of Job's good fortune, and mine, that he was a member of a wealthy family, a fact that became increasingly obvious as plans proceeded. I was overjoyed that he managed to purchase a location for us which nurtured fig and date trees and our own olive trees. He described for me an altogether beautiful setting. Most of all, I loved knowing that the land encompassed several precious acacia trees. Because acacia trees are used for smelting copper ore as well as for building, they are very much in demand, so it was truly a luxury to have our own just to give us pleasure.

Arching from a solid trunk, the branches of the acacia tree rise gradually outward and upward to provide wonderful cool shade in the hottest days of summer, much better than the protection of our tents, which seemed to trap old heat inside. But more than that, their flowing shapes, always firm and solid and constant, still change from season to season as their surroundings bathe them in different colors. A burning pink against the yellow fire of the high heat of summer, they seem to turn a deep orange and rust when summer begins to turn to winter. And sometimes, they herald an approaching storm in their mauve and black against a brown sky.

More than that, I believed that acacia trees were blessed with a special kind of spirit. My Astarte's beautiful breasts were carved from the hard wood of the acacia tree, wood which also held up our tents and provided fire to warm us in the winter. I knew that Astarte, in her wisdom, had provided the earth with deep suckling breasts for the roots of the acacia trees, who could reach deep into the ground to the water far below. That is why they survived so well even in times of drought. I knew Astarte would bless our marriage in the same deep and lasting way.

Once Job had described the setting of our future home, I could hardly wait to see it. Of course I wanted to share that joy with Adah. It was a full day's distance from my family's location, so it was not an easy project getting there. But my family put together a traveling group to pay a visit to the home of Uncle

Mrs. Job

Ruel and my future mother-in-law, close by Job's property. Two of my sisters, a few of their older children, two of my brothers-in-law, and one of my brothers escorted Adah and me, traveling by donkey, sometimes riding the beasts and sometimes walking beside them.

The journey was almost as exciting as my betrothal ceremony had been and my anticipated wedding would be. Somehow, on the trip, I was especially aware of the beauty of the land. We passed groves of sycamore trees rising full and thick from their wide bases on the ground, gleaming white in reflected sunlight, with leaves both silver and green protecting the rose-red figs. The groves came to life with shepherds who were busy piercing the skin of the fruit so it would ripen. Further on, there were clusters of spiny thistle with its pink flowers. At one point, we passed a huge wind-shaped mushroom, its large head standing out against the pink and yellowish-tan starkness of the desert around it. Further on, I was bathed in nostalgia as we saw in the distance a field of the pink rock rose that had provided the scent of the oil Uncle Ruel had given our dolls many years before. Everything seemed so bright and beautiful as to be unreal. My exhilaration was almost beyond containment.

Arriving at Uncle Ruel's long, deep tent, ebony black from the color of the sheep whose hair had provided its fabric and deepened over time by the action of the sun, we were greeted with a celebration of music and food that none of us had anticipated. As the servants laid out the elaborate feast, musicians appeared with goatskin bags fitted out to provide music. They blew on a short thin bone to swell the bag with air, which was then squeezed in and out while a tone was created by fingering the holes in a longer bone on the other side of the instrument. Their heavy tones supported the lightness of the flutes and harps, while the clapping together of elaborately carved ivory sticks spelled out an irresistible rhythm. The joyful surprise swelled into swirls of dancing and laughter. My ecstatic pleasure was tempered only by the thought that things couldn't possibly get any better—that my wedding day might seem less by comparison.

In the midst of the merriment, we filtered off in small groups to see the location of my future home with Job. It was even lovelier than I had anticipated, the trees and surrounding fields of wild flowers seeming magical. Oh how thankful I was for Astarte's blessing! Job tried to draw our future tent for me in my imagination, but I was too taken with the location to even want to bother to imagine more.

There was room for most of our party to sojourn in Uncle Ruel's ample tent that night, but his servants had also raised another one on his property for some of the men to stay. The welcome could not have been any more wonderful. Equally grand was the morning feast he provided before seeing us off to return home the next day.

We hadn't been on our way very long, however, when I felt my attention drawn away from the beauty of all that I had seen and enjoyed on this journey.

My chest is feeling so tight. It is so hard to breath, like a sandstorm is on its way. Oh, Astarte, guide us to the safety of home before it attacks us.

I looked around me, expecting to see everyone gathering speed to get to safety before the storm came. Strangely, they were all still laughing and making music as if nothing troublesome were happening.

It is so hard to breathe. The atmosphere is pressing against my chest. I do not want to die now. Everything has been so beautiful. To be exposed to a sandstorm would be a terrible thing. All my dreams of marriage and joy may not come true. I cannot seem to breathe in enough air. Why is everyone else ignoring the signs?

Only Adah was subdued. I kept my fears to myself, confused as I listened to the singing and laughter of my companions. My body focused on trying to take in enough air. I just wanted to get home safe.

Strangely, even when I mentioned the weather change after we arrived home, no one else admitted having experienced it. Only Adah seemed to feel it.

My family began preparing my wedding clothes. Job's family was doing that for him, too, because for our wedding we would be really dressed up, king and queen for a week, you might say. Now it was time for Job's father to pay my father the dowry they had agreed on. Partly that was to make up for the fact that I would no longer be around to work for the family, but it was a kind of protection for me too, because even though my father could use it, the assumption was that some of it would be available for me in case I should become widowed or divorced.

It was also time for my father to give me the gifts he had agreed on. Part of that dowry consisted of gold coins that were made into a circlet for my marriage headpiece. All in all, it was a pretty expensive proposition for my family. I began to realize why Job and I would want sons rather than daughters, who would cost a lot and eventually leave the family. Even though dowries might be expensive, sons would remain in the family to continue working. And the children Job and I would have would be part of his family's heritage, not mine. That did not mean my parents had no love for the children my sisters already had and would not love the ones I would birth. But the fact is that daughters are of less value in terms of wealth.

As we moved toward our wedding day, I felt less and less like a child. My time with Adah was spent differently, both of us talking about family and children and responsibility—not playing at it, but planning for it.

"You will see, Adah; things will not be very different for us. My home will still be your second home, just as it has always been, and your home will still be mine."

Adah made no response.

If our betrothal day had been special, it was nothing compared to the emotions the wedding preparations evoked in me. I began to feel like royalty about to be crowned queen. I had seen my sisters and other young women in our settlement travel this route to marriage, but this time the focus was on me. I admit I felt really important—and nervous! I was afraid of our wedding night. Suddenly, the anticipation of lovemaking was not some kind of vague dream, but a challenge—to enjoy it? To do it right? Playing at pregnancy and childbirth was giving way to fears that I would not have the traditional strength of the women in my family. I could die giving birth. I could be barren. Would Job stay with me then? Would he divorce me? Would he turn his love and attention to other wives? To concubines? Would I ever come to know the "potage love" my mother described? The anxiety did not terminate my excitement, but it was an ever-flowing, contaminating undercurrent.

As for the fear of my wedding night, my three married sisters were of very little help. One sister was almost poetic about how great it would be; another tried to cheer me up by telling me it would not be so bad after the first lovemaking; and a third just complained that the other two should let me find out for myself.

I was not concerned about being happy with Job. I did fear that I might do something to spoil things, but I was confident that Job would be the ideal husband. Sometimes I did wonder, though, if he knew enough about lovemaking to get past my total ignorance.

Chapter Five: The Consummation

So, the activities of the preparation year went on. Job was busy, with the help of his family, preparing our marriage tent. It would be a traditional tent, made of goats'-hair fabric held up by stakes of acacia wood, but, because it was erected for permanence, it could have several rooms. There would be a central section generally open on one side, but with a flap that could be closed to protect from sand- and windstorms, as well as an occasional driving rain. That was a kind of porch where most of daily life would go on, cooking, entertaining guests.

In the beginning, there would be two more sections, each set off from the main section by hangings, which would be beautifully bright and colorful, mostly the creative work of my family. Some hangings, however, would be purchased, like the rugs for the floors, from passing merchants. One room would be for women only. Job would be the only man allowed to enter there. The other room would be sleeping quarters, initially for Job and me, but also for the children who would come, and sometimes for guests. Someday, there would be outlying tents for the servants and slaves, but Job was not yet able to acquire such help. We would get to share with his parents, however, a fact which would alter my life more than I anticipated.

There was an urgent necessity to get the basic tent constructed before the rains of early winter came, because until the goats' hair got wet, it would leak. Once it rained, the fabric would close up and it would be waterproof. Only after that could household items be kept inside and dry.

Even as our future home became firm, my body became more mature. The commitment had been made, and the time for our wedding approached. From then on, it was all tradition and ritual which swept us along as if it had a will of its own. Scared and awed as we may have been, there was never any thought of turning back.

The air shuddered with anticipation as my family acquired cooking and storage pots and busily wove blankets and additional decorative hangings for my home. The garments I had worn for my betrothal celebration, too small for me to wear now, had been taken apart, bleached in the sun, re-dyed, and torn into strips from which my mother wove a deep blue and green blanket to cover Job and me in our marital tent. When I saw it, I did briefly remember my doll, wrapped in her own blue and green blanket, but my thoughts quickly laid her aside. More wonderful than any doll was the lovely Astarte my mother had attained to bless my home. Created differently from the Astarte I would be leaving behind at my mother's home, her reddish yellow ample breasts and full hips were formed of pottery clay. Her presence would guarantee my success at birthing many children for Job.

At the time, my attention was completely on Job and me and our coming marriage, so I did not really appreciate that this wedding of mine was a triumph for my entire clan. My father had negotiated a very successful union in joining me to Uncle Ruel's family. As a consequence, my extended family, always traditionally involved in marriage preparations, worked even more diligently and excitedly to prepare for my wedding.

Extraordinary attention was paid to the preparation of my bridal garments, dazzling in their vivid, joyful colors. The linen undergarment was, of course, particularly soft to the touch, having been carefully prepared by the loving hands of my truly skilled mother. To the eye, it was a thrust of brilliant yellow. When the gaze traveled to the arms, however, even that color paled against the brilliance of the full sleeves, beaded in translucent carnelian of blood red, orange, peach, and pomegranate rose, along with agate combinations of black, brown, and milky white, and occasional bronze and gold.

It was not only the beading that made the sleeves of such great consequence, but just the fact of full sleeves themselves. They were a mark of wealth, for only women tended by slaves and servants could wear them. They would just get in the way of ordinary nomads doing their daily work. The sleeves were a temporary tribute to Job and me as to any bride and groom who live for a week like true royalty. Nor would the jewels remain in my possession after the time of wedding celebration. Most were borrowed, supplementing the few that were owned by my family. For us nomadic women, our marriage feast would be the only time we would expect ever to wear long, full sleeves. Just like the wedding, it was a special symbol to be enjoyed only once. The sleeves would be removed and the jewels returned to their various owners. I could plan, however, to keep the soft, bright yellow undergarment, without the sleeves, for special occasions.

There is more to describe, a task which helps me keep alive the memory of that time when I felt more vital and significant than ever before or since. Sometimes when everything turns gray, I am revived by the memory of the splendor of those colors and those days. Now I know it was not so much the shades and tints of the events themselves, but the pigments with which my eyes dyed them. How fortunate it is to live the days at hand without seeing what is to come.

And so to continue the description of my glorious wedding attire. Over the bright yellow undergarment was a slightly shorter deep red tunic, and around my waist was a bronze orange girdle—a kind of wide belt also adorned with precious stones. Even my sandals were jeweled. My veil, dyed and woven by my mother in a blue so deep it was almost purple, rivaled any that the wealthiest of women might wear. Circled by the crown of gold from my father, it would cover my face at the beginning of the ceremony. It is not that Job did not know what I looked like, of course, but it was tradition for me to be presented covered at our bridal ceremony.

Probably because my family was so skilled in the use of color, my eldest sister had developed a rather uncommon ability to create design with henna. She made me a gift of that art on both my hands and my feet. Although black when she applied it, over a short time, the henna turned to a vibrant bronze. Never again would anyone spend so much time touching my hands and my feet. She spent a whole day not long before my wedding applying the henna so it would be just the right color and last through the early days of my marriage. On my feet and ankles, she applied a lovely intricate pattern. But more exciting to me was what she gave my hands. On the palms, in the center of a lavish design, she sketched a pomegranate, one of the sacrifices Astarte was most pleased to receive, and on the back of my hands was another of my dear goddess's favorites, a sheep. I was overjoyed to know that my hands, touching Job, would be offering devotion to Astarte at the same time. It helped to reduce somewhat my fears of the wedding night.

And so came the day of our wedding. After a full bath, one of the few I could expect to have in my lifetime, I was covered with precious oils bought especially for the occasion. My long, black hair was bound and covered by my jeweled veil, thrown back from my face until time for the marriage rites. My face was rouged and my eyes darkened. Needless to say, I had never felt so special, with all the women in my family bustling about to make me gorgeous, nor did I expect ever again to feel so well attended.

Job, at the temporary quarters where he and his retinue sojourned outside the area of our camp, was receiving the same care, even being adorned in precious jewels as well. Knowing the attention he was receiving, I should have expected it, but he still caused me to gasp with joy when he and his family arrived at our tent early that morning. His whole family looked splendid, as did mine. His eldest brother, serving as the "friend of the bridegroom," was magnificent. Looking at him, as at his father, Uncle Ruel, I knew I could expect that my Job would retain his handsome appearance for many years.

I was reminded of the caution with which Job and I approached, and at the same time, avoided, each other on the day of our betrothal. Now, again, I felt some of the same strangeness, but it was tinged with a different kind of comfort in knowing that we would be riding side by side to our own home after this ritual. There would be a different newness to overcome, and a new joy in accomplishing it.

A very formal affair followed. I was accompanied by my two beautifully dressed "companions," Adah on one side and my eldest sister on the other. Job and his brother stood apart, waiting for me to be led to them. After the exchange of the gifts that had been promised at the time of our betrothal, my father led me to Job, removing my veil and putting it on Job's shoulder, saying, "The government is on your shoulders."

I wonder how it felt to my father when he did that, basically giving me away. I know I was close to crying, not only from joy.

Then Uncle Ruel said to me something like, "May you be blessed with a full and happy life and many healthy children."

Adah was given the honor of placing on my head our tribe's bright beaded wedding crown as a sign that I was now a married woman. A stunning piece, weighted by precious stones and with bejeweled bands hanging down around the head and face, it would be mine to wear for the week of our wedding celebration. I know Adah was looking at it with joyful anticipation, aware that soon she would be happily wearing it after her marriage to Narmer.

I confess that I was paying very little attention to the larger group that surrounded us, so I was a bit startled when Eliphaz, Uncle Ruel's elderly relative, stepped forward.

"It is my pleasure to represent the hope of the entire clan that your marriage will be fruitful and long-lasting."

Then he presented me with a beaded gold necklace.

"This gold represents the protection of your entire family, to be yours in times of joy and times of sorrow, in times of hope and in times of fear, always to belong to you alone so that you may never be poor."

Then he embraced me, kissing me first on one cheek and then on the other.

It was rather stiffly formal. When I saw how people had stepped aside to make ample room for his passage, I realized that he was a very important man, due a great deal of respect as a wise elder. I was honored that such a personage had traveled the long distance from his own country to be here, but I think I felt less awe than the others, probably because I was too busy paying attention to Job.

Following this ceremony, we enjoyed some refreshment—fruit, cheese, wheat bread, and some beer. It was necessary to give us sustenance for the journey ahead. But the real feast and celebration awaited our arrival at our new home, a day's journey away, a journey that began when Job and I mounted the camels provided by his father and mine.

If Job and I were feeling like royalty, I wanted to imagine that our camels did too. Their colorful protective blankets rivaled anything that had ridden into our camp in the past. In fact, taking in the entire group traveling with us, there was every color and jewel one might imagine, with the exception of purple, far too scarce and expensive for the likes of us nomads. When my camel knelt low enough for my father to help me board him, it was almost as if he were praying. I wanted to believe that he was pleading with Astarte to protect our journey. I certainly was offering that plea. Oh, of course I know he was just doing what he had been trained to do, but it was very hard on that day not to feel like everything in the world had been put there just for

Job and me. We certainly did tower above most of those traveling with us.

Once the entire party was gathered, we proceeded toward our new home. As many people as possible traveled with us in celebration. Not all could afford to be away from their flocks and fields. For those we left behind, there was enough food and beer to provide a feast when they returned. On the entire journey, we were accompanied by music and singing, even more joyful than we had experienced on the earlier occasion when we visited Uncle Ruel's. As we approached our home, I dismounted and joined the dancing. So many times, my body had been restless with fear or anticipation. This time, my body swayed in harmony with my joy, spiritedly in a rhythmic beat of heart and mind as one, so much in unity that I truly thought not at all about what I was doing as the spirit carried me along.

Fortunately, the heat was not the intense golden waves of summer, undulating ceaselessly and feverishly toward the sky. It was more constant now, almost relaxed, as the first part of winter celebrated the planting of the crops and the calmer time of waiting. Warm, carefree, eager, and full, we approached our new life together.

Once we arrived in the area where Uncle Ruel and Job occupied so much of the land, I began to feel the surging waves of heat that were not there on our journey. No one else was aware of them, except perhaps Job might have been experiencing them too. They were raging inside me, interfering with my appetite for all the glorious foods being offered by Uncle Ruel's servants. To be fair, there was one other person who seemed to know the turmoil that was going on in my belly. Aunt Beta, who was now my mother-in-law, served me a goblet of grape juice even as she laid her hand on my shoulder. Never one to talk much, she spoke kindness and comfort with her gesture. I found myself giving in to the message that we would live well together, now that I was to be her daughter, perhaps more than my own mother's, given the distance we would be living from my old home.

My body joined the feast. And what a banquet it was! So much more lavish than even the most wonderful traditional celebratory meals we nomads were usually able to bring together. The music trembled in my face and ears, and the dancing was a pulsation so complete that I had no thought of what I was doing. Every once in a while, Adah and I found each other to exchange excited hugs. Even Jarna was there, shyly enfolding me. In fact, it seemed that everyone was hugging me—and Job. I was happily lost in the ecstasy of this time and place toward which we had all been working for a year.

Then time vanished; darkness began to close in, and I suddenly felt a powerful urge to seek out Adah and embrace her with a river of tears in which she joined, which surprised both of us. No words were necessary. We knew then that we would never have the same relationship again. Something vital to both of us was over, though I knew that we would be deep friends forever, even though apart. Still, there was grief in this moment of parting.

Just at that point, Job came up behind me and nudged me gently on the elbow. Sharp bolts of fear, regret, and anticipation burst inside me. I did not want to leave Adah, nor end the merriment. I envied all those with us who were free to go on with the feast. I wanted to go with Job. I did not want to go with Job. I cannot apply a label to what I was feeling. I did know that the goal had been reached and I missed the striving. Now there was a new purpose.

Job guided me into our private quarters. I saw the lovely deep bed of straw, covered by the bleached white bedclothes we would have to stain to prove my virginity. The private feast laid out for us in one section did nothing to relieve the panic that seized me. I had thought Job and I were the center of attention during this whole time of preparation and celebration. Now I knew it had been nothing but a distraction to prevent my thinking of what was about to happen. Job and I were left alone to be the focus of each other's lives.

Mrs. Job

My dread was worse than anything I had ever experienced in anticipation of the possibility of enemies raiding our camp. And it was different, made worse by some kind of hopeful excitement about what we were doing alone together in this place. I wanted to turn around and run back out to the celebration that was still going on. I envied friends and family out there who did not have to experience what I was going through.

Job stood behind me, knowing, I guess, something of what I was feeling. Maybe he was feeling it too. Whispering, "Don't be afraid," he touched my shoulder, evoking a spark that blazed straight on down to my toes. Then he removed the crown from my head, replacing the weight of it with a throbbing circlet of elation that swirled around my brow and spiraled down through the most private parts of my body. It was almost intolerably breathtaking when he released my hair from the beads that contained it and fingered it as it fell.

Engulfed by an eddy of unimagined, wonderfully frightening sensations, I turned around to see Job, as if expecting some kind of stabilizing comfort. There, for the first time, facing each other fully, we were joined. He was my husband. I reached out to uncover those glistening muscles I had yearned to touch so long ago. Fear was gone. I know we folded our elegant garments carefully and put them aside, but I can't fully recount the route of our early "pomegranate and figs and special cheese" love, culminating in the deep, yet ecstatic agony as his body filled mine. I think I cried out in pain. I think we laughed some.

The dancing and music continued long into the night and even into the next day. I felt no envy for those outside our tent. No love, I was sure, had ever been as intense as ours. And it was sealed as I finally drifted off to sleep, Job's words giving my body a final caress.

"I am glad our fathers arranged our marriage."

The next morning, we woke up together and alone in our private room in our own tent. One of my first thoughts was of my sister, who complained that the other two should let me find out for myself what my first night with Job would be like. She was right. Unlike the preparations that went into making us ready for our wedding, only Job and I could create our marriage.

I felt relieved, deeply happy, and very grown-up, but also, strangely, a little sad. I had never before been alone with just one person. It struck me that our life would be like this for a while, at least until we had children. On the other hand, I had never been joined with anyone the way Job and I now were.

We were really married, and we had the bloody bedclothes to show for it. It was time to dress again in our ceremonial clothes and present the evidence to my mother, who proudly, with the help of the whole family, paraded it before the crowd.

So, the hard—and wonderful—part had been done. I had expected that we could now give the week-long celebration our complete attention, but it did not happen that way. Our first night together had wrapped us in ourselves and each other in a way that tended to block out concern for what was going on around us. I felt a kind of power I had never felt before—not easily described—a kind of being solid from head to toe, yet bold at the same time. There were many times when I would have been happy to leave the crowd to return to our section of the tent with Job. And my attention focused often on the new sensations where Job had broken into my body. Truthfully, I was experiencing pain, but it felt to me like a secret tribute. I wondered if people could read all these feelings on my face.

Then it was all over, suddenly, even shockingly. The party ended; the celebrants returned to their homes; and I was part of a new family and a new way of life.

The depth of loneliness was far greater than I had anticipated. Not only did I miss my own family, and Adah, and the others who traveled with us, I missed the very duties that had been the essence of my daily life. Uncle Ruel and my mother-in-law were surrounded by servants and slaves who performed the daily chores. I was not needed to mill the grain, or make the bread, or sweep the floors, or prepare the evening potage, or carry food to those tending the flocks, or tease the wool, or separate the layers of flax, or pull the weeds, or even to help plant the seeds.

I realized that my mother had known how great the difference would be when she provided my home with the basic necessities for dyeing and weaving. Spinning was an occupation which I could pursue as well. Aunt Beta, in her quiet way, also understood. I imagine her life was quite different from the nomadic existence she and Uncle Ruel had experienced when they were first married. For her, the change occurred gradually, not so abruptly as it did for me, so she had a chance to adapt to it a little at a time.

At any rate, she did her best to introduce me into my new way of life and to the important, though different, functions I would perform. The very first morning, after Job had gone out to supervise the care of his flocks, she invited me to ride out with her.

"Come with me, Dara. We will visit the tents of those who serve our family."

I recognized that this was the first day of my training in how to be Job's wife. How different it would be from what I had witnessed in my own home. I was afraid.

How can I possibly meet Aunt Beta's expectations? I don't belong here.

She must have read my mind.

"Dara, you will find this strange at first, but all you have to do is listen, remember what is said, and do what has to be done."

Each place we stopped, it was clear people were happy to see her. Mostly, we found women caring for small children, running happily about, mostly unclothed, copying—and thereby learning—their mother's chores. I felt at home. I also admired the gentle way in which my mother-in-law took the children into her arms.

At each stop, she inquired about the needs of the people we saw, clearly making mental note of the requests. At some stops, she delivered items such as water jars, rugs, bed coverings, and even some clothing. Some of what she left with the recipients would be used for bartering. Others would be more directly useful. I could see that they were all responses to past requests that she found appropriate.

I have not appreciated Aunt Beta's power. Just because she is so quiet in Uncle Ruel's presence, I haven't noticed much about her except her jewelry. I was wrong. She has set me quite a challenge.

I learned as I became a more intimate part of the family that the cloth she provided was the product of her own hand.

This is good. I can certainly do as well as she does in the task of weaving.

I felt a sense of personal pride and accomplishment knowing I had the skill to make beautiful fabrics. Feeling a bit better about my own ability to carry out the obligations of being Job's wife, I was able to enjoy my mother-in-law without apprehension.

I confess, though, that my thoughts were constantly with Job, enduring frequent stabs of longing for him. I could hardly wait to unite with him over the evening meal, which we did share at his parents' lavish tent. Even more, I wanted the day to end so I could be alone with him in our own home. My mother's description of a "figs-and-pomegranates-and-special-cheeses" love hardly did justice to my feelings for my husband.

Still, I had not anticipated longing so much for my own people, a pang which struck me every evening at mealtime. I even missed the barley bread, rarely provided by Job's parents, who could afford wheat on a regular basis. I missed the conversation, and I missed the *V* of my father's legs as he squatted to hold me. I missed being a child even as I took joy in being a married woman.

I had been in my new home about a week when my mother-in-law ordered a sheep to be sacrificed to my Astarte. It was always Aunt Beta's function to order the slaughter of animals when appropriate, but this sacrifice, I recognized, was a special tribute to me. I think she recognized my longing for my old home, and perhaps even feared that I might lose my dedication to her son. She need not have worried about the latter possibility. Nonetheless, I was touched at the special homage to my goddess.

Loneliness dwindled some with time, and I settled into a kind of routine, enjoying the company of the women of Job's family. The sense of being alone in a new world often attacked me, however, when I was weaving, a task which was becoming a major function and source of pride for me. I wanted to be with my own very talented family then.

The truth is, marriage did change my life in ways that struck me to the core. I was still constantly busy on a daily basis, but with tasks that were new to me. Gradually, my mother-in-law taught me the skill of assessing the value of land which might potentially be purchased as well as flocks that might be added to Uncle Ruel's wealth. What I was learning would add to my value as Job's wife.

Always in the back of my mind during the early months of my marriage, or maybe more often in the forefront, was the expectation that I would soon be with child. Then, I believed, I would feel that I was really becoming useful as a wife to Job and as a member of his family. I even thought I would feel more accepted by all of them as one who truly belonged.

Strangely, when I finally was pregnant, I failed to recognize it right away. I knew I could expect my monthly bleeding to stop when I was pregnant, and I certainly knew that my body would eventually swell with the fullness of the child inside, but I had not expected the subtle feelings I had in the beginning. Some of it I cannot even describe, but I do know my breasts began to harden a bit, and I was surprised when Job's touch caused them pain. My legs felt more burdened, which made no sense to me, because in the beginning, they bore no more weight than usual. And my pelvis felt—well—strange, as if someone had inserted a tiny pebble which weighed on me. At first, I thought it was just more of the effects of my frequent lovemaking with Job. Thanks to being with the women, though, I felt free to talk about my feelings, and they were quick to rejoice that I was with child.

After all, childbearing is a primary and desirable function for wives. Actually, I think one or two of the older women knew just by looking at me, even in the early weeks. I was finally totally convinced when I felt a little sick in the mornings, though I must say that part was not very bothersome for me.

I was happy. Now I was really a fully mature woman, worthy of all the respect that goes with it. Well, almost. I still needed the final seal of actually giving birth. Marriage had taken me out of childhood, pregnancy had taken me well along the road, but the final confirmation of my full value as a woman would be when I actually gave birth to a healthy baby. Of course, I would feel especially wonderful if I gave birth to a boy.

I confess, though, that I also felt fear—fear that I might fail at giving birth, that I might birth the baby too soon, before it could survive out in the world, or that I might give birth to an unhealthy child. I did not allow myself to be aware of it often, but I was also afraid I might die. I tried but could not totally stop myself from rehearsing the reasons to be anxious, even terrified. There were women in our tribe who died in childbirth, and there were babies born dead.

All the mothers around me understood that experience of frightened joy, and, of course, Job's family, like my own, had developed many practices to help assure success and just keep me focused on the hope. I guess the most important thing they did for me was what they did *not* do. They did not treat my pregnancy like it was some kind of special event. I mean, they just took it for granted that I would be successful, and with that kind of confidence around me, it was easier to be calm. Astarte was a great comfort to me too; I felt that my prayers would be answered by her protection, especially because Aunt Beta was constant in her offerings of sacrifice to Astarte.

Part of the reassurance was found in our rules about how to be pregnant. Especially there were traditions about food. That makes sense, of course, because obviously the developing child would be sharing my food to help it grow. At the same time, it needed to be spared foods that might cause it a problem. I was specifically warned to avoid salt and fat, both of which were felt to be dangerous for the baby. Even depriving myself of those foods swelled my sense of pride in what was going on in my body. Like my betrothal, and later my marriage, I knew I was not the first or only one to have the experience. But this was happening to me, and that was very different from observing it in others.

Otherwise, and surprisingly, life went on as usual while I grew larger and heavier. When I say heavy, I mean specifically that sensation of the little pebble becoming a rock dragging down inside me as the pregnancy progressed. No one had told me, either, that I would wake in the night with terrible cramps in my legs, or that my baby would heartlessly and almost constantly beat on me as if angry for being restrained in its inner prison. All in all, when it finally came time to deliver my baby, I was more than ready.

It was time for Job's first child to enter the world.

Chapter Six: Fruitful and Multiplying

I was almost fourteen years old when the pains began. I guess there is no better time to be surrounded by a tent full of women than when the agony starts. And I do mean agony. I had heard other women screaming, but there was no knowing the real pain until I experienced it for myself. They told me I did some shrieking too, and I guess that helped to ease some of the tension inside, but I honestly do not remember that. Probably I was too busy hurting to hear what I was doing. The interesting thing is that now I can tell about the birthing, but I cannot really remember the full depth of it. I guess if it had stayed with me in all of its suffering, I would have been more than terrified when I went through my other pregnancies.

Knowing that I was about ready, we had made some preparations in the women's section of our tent. We had already piled up some large stones, covered by rugs for comfort, for my hips to rest on when pushing the baby out. The rugs were firm, soft, and new, created by my mother and aunts specifically for the birthing of my first child. They had chosen the soothing colors of green and blue, with a bit of yellow and orange mixed in to reflect the excitement and change surrounding the event. Offerings had been made to Astarte to help facilitate a healthy delivery, and strips of clean linen had been set aside, along with the aromatic oil purchased just for this birth. I had chosen the aroma of the pink rock rose, the gift Uncle Ruel had given Adah and me many years ago for our dolls. I loved the scent, but I think also it was a way of bringing my childhood with me into this final move into adulthood. With all the preparation, and with a lifetime of living with women, I was not surprised by what came next, but I certainly was not fully prepared. Once again, there was the truth that this time I was not just watching. It was happening to me.

My mother had begun the journey to my home as soon as she received the word from one of Uncle Ruel's servants that I was about to give birth. I was greatly relieved when she joined my mother-in-law, Aunt Beta, inside the tent. She brought with her a wave of relief and a sense of safety. She also brought pomegranates to offer in sacrifice to Astarte, who was watching over the whole process from a corner of the tent.

My mothers kept me walking around, even though I begged to lie down, while the heat seemed to be roaring into the tent from outside and straight to my body. As my married sisters and sisters-in-law joined us, they took on the task of bathing my face and even my body in cool water and oils.

I do not want to make too much of it, but I certainly did enjoy the pauses when the cramping pain let up on its seizing. On the other hand, when the pangs started coming closer together, I was relieved, and so were the women around me, I think.

Finally, it was time. I think we nomads had an advantage in that we spent so much of our time sitting cross-legged on the ground, or squatting, so we did have very strong legs. And that certainly helped when I was digging my feet deep into the ground as I alternately pushed and relaxed the baby's way out. The pillars of stone we had constructed supported my hips on both sides, leaving space for the baby to emerge. My mother stood behind me, basically leaning her own body against my back; the other women in the room took turns massaging the area where the baby would emerge; and my mother-in-law stood ready to receive her grandchild when it was born. Then, as I felt the most intense, tight, painful, cramping binding around my lower abdomen, the women in the room began to get excited, urging me to push. I just wanted to die, but I did press down, almost unthinkingly obeying their instructions.

And then it happened. My first son was born. What happy sounds of celebration and relief came from the women's tent. I suppose it must have been hard for Job outside with the other men waiting to get the word, but I imagine he was relieved, too, that the sounds were happy. The baby could not be presented to him until the women had washed him with water, bathed him in the special oil, and wrapped him tight in the strips of linen cloth to help him grow firm and straight. Then Job's mother had the honor of bringing the baby out to him with the announcement, "This is your son." The men cheered as Job raised his firstborn high in the air and gave him his name. "He will be known as Primus, Son of Job." Of course, after he and the men around him had welcomed our boy into the world, Job returned his son to his mother, who brought him back into the tent.

In the meantime, I had been through the birthing process again. This time, it was nowhere near so painful, but more of a surprise to me, because I had not really understood about the afterbirth, when all that part inside me that had cradled my baby was now expelled.

What pain? Already, I could hardly remember what I had just endured. My eldest sister placed the baby to my breast, and he began to suck the liquid that came before anything that really looked like milk. Now the sensations were different. First of all, I felt so light and unburdened. Most of all, I knew the wonderful tickle/tingle in my breasts and my pelvis as the baby drew the life-giving fluid from my nipples. How he did suck! It seemed that he would follow the tradition of Job's family and mine and be a really healthy child.

When all was complete, and I was cleaned, I lay down on the bed of rugs and blankets the women had prepared for me. I would rest for a while as my breasts filled with hearty milk for my son.

If I did not have enough for him, he would be brought to a wet nurse. I did not want that to happen, so I rested and ate the good foods my sisters brought to me, even those prepared with the fat and salt of which I had been deprived while I was pregnant.

Once little Primus had settled into a calm sleep, Job was allowed to come in. He was so happy; he even said so. And what a carefully warm and loving hug he gave me. We definitely had not yet reached the "potage" stage of our love. On the other hand, I really wanted no thought of his getting close to me with anything more than his warm embrace. It is a good thing tradition required a long period before we could share a bed again.

I know some women worried that their husbands would go to a concubine at this point, but I had no fear of that with Job. I knew he was faithful to me. Even more important, he was so wrapped up in joy and pride over his son that it was hard for him to think of anything else. Just as I was now feeling like a complete woman, I knew he was feeling whole as a man. My mother was right. There was an amazing shared intimate joy in the birth of our first child. Job and I had become flesh of each other's flesh through marriage; now that oneness was sealed with this little sleeping fusion of our selves.

Only one thing was needed to make this day complete, and I asked Job about it.

"When is my friend Adah coming?"

One of my first thoughts when the pain began to seize me had been to ask someone to fetch Adah. Given the distance between us, we saw very little of each other since we both married.

"My sister Tiva traveled with some of my father's servants to fetch her."

I was so grateful to Tiva and so anxious to see Adah. The truth was that her very presence would make everything seem complete. My love for Job was intense and all-encompassing, but it was different from the deep devotion Adah and I had developed in all the years of growing together.

Shortly after I had drifted into a comfortable sleep, I was awakened by an increased intensity of the sounds of people outside our tent. The voices had become louder and more high-pitched as they welcomed Tiva back, escorting Adah. I think many of the family and their servants were happy for me, pleased to think that I was being given this gift of a visit from my old friend. Now my birthing was complete. Adah was here to celebrate the reality of what had been play for us for so many years.

The months apart had made some changes. Adah was still attired in the off-white and brown of our daily nomadic costume, but her face was changed, mostly because there was added bulk in her cheeks. Her eyes even looked different—tired, and yet more brilliantly alive. I realized with joy as my gaze moved on down to her belly that it was full. I wondered if my face and eyes had displayed such changes when I was growing Primus inside me.

Adah's presence bathed me in a sense of totally comfortable completeness. After all, had our lives not been built on the anticipation of these moments of birth? Knowing that she was about to join me in motherhood brought our friendship full circle. I was contented for myself and our relationship and very happy for her.

We exchanged a long, tight embrace, and I asked her, "How long will it be before you give birth?"

"Another month, Dara, so I guess once again, you have moved ahead of me."

Then, of course, she wanted all the details of my birthing process—shared intimately and comfortably with her as I could do with no other.

Adah sojourned with us for a night, staying with me in the women's section of the tent. It was easy for us to become like little girls again, remembering our play and adventures. When Adah joined me in making a thank offering to Astarte, we could not help giggling, remembering the time we had offered her a sheep of mud. In between we were both happy to doze and eventually to drift into a deep sleep through the night.

She began the journey back to her own home the next day, escorted by some of Uncle Ruel's servants and bearing hopes for a healthy birth. She also carried a supply of food that Job insisted on sending with her. At first she seemed a little insulted, until we reminded her of the law of hospitality. I wondered why she reacted the way she did, but Job seemed to understand.

"Adah did not want to accept charity from us. Think of it; we do have so much more than Narmer's family does."

Job was generous, not only in giving, but in tactful understanding.

Uncle Ruel could not enter the women's tent, but when I finally emerged from my confinement, he was right there waiting, with one of his big hugs for me—and the gift of a gold bracelet. Primus was by no means his first grandson, but he seemed as happy as if this were a first for him. My father was happy too, mostly because he was relieved that I had survived well and his new grandson was healthy and lovable. The wealth, so to speak, was Uncle Ruel's, but the gain of loving offspring belonged to both of them. I was a very fortunate woman.

It was almost two months later that I received word from someone passing through our town that Adah had given birth to a healthy boy. I was delighted. We were two friends making our way through life together, though apart. I left immediately to join her in celebration. Job and I prepared bags of gifts for her and the baby, and I rode off, escorted by a couple of Job's sisters. I was particularly pleased to be bringing a lovely blanket I had woven especially for Adah's child.

Adah seemed happy, and maybe a little surprised, to see me.

"How could I not have been happy for you, Adah?"

She received our gifts with polite and rather formal thanks, giving special favor to the blanket I had made.

"How lovely to have a gift of your own making. All the others are nice and appreciated, but they come from Job's wealth. This comes from your heart—and hands."

Adah brought up the memory of all the times I had been annoyed with my mother because she wanted me to card or spin when I wanted to weave.

"Remember how good you were, Dar', at angry outbursts? They were funny to watch, though a little scary, and not at all nice when I was the object of them."

I did not understand how the topic of anger was raised so quickly upon my arrival, but it did lead us into the pleasure of recalling our childhood.

"I guess I was too prone to anger, Adah, but I think partly it was because I had a strong sense of fairness. And in a way, I suppose my mother encouraged me, because she usually took the time to find out what was behind my outrage."

We drifted into reminiscing and laughing about our early years. I loved my life with Job and my new family and friends, but there would never be anything like what Adah and I had shared.

Adah was no longer in confinement, so I did not get to sleep alone with her as she had with me. She had returned to Narmer's bed. But there was a warm welcome for Job's sisters and me to sleep in the women's portion of the tent. Over the evening potage and before our departure the next morning, Adah and I had time together to share more of our stories with Job's sisters. I left feeling nourished with the love of an old friend.

Primus's birth had brought a change to our household which pleased me. Our lives became more centered in our own tent, and for a while, the skills I had learned in growing up were put to use again as I prepared the evening potage, swept the tent, and even sometimes milled the flour. There was comfort for me in that.

Our family continued to be fruitful. True to my heritage, I was good at childbearing. During the next fifteen years, I birthed nine more healthy children, two of whom were twins. I received the help of all the people who were involved in raising our children as the way things had always been. I only vaguely realized that wealth and power were becoming an accepted way of life for Job and me, not just a sharing of his father's wealth.

For our firstborn children, the services of the wet nurses had been gifts from Job's parents, freeing me to engage in the business of our family and allowing my body to prepare itself for further pregnancies. Increasingly, our later children were cared for by our own servants. Our whole household, family and servants alike, however, was like family, largely because of Job's kind and tactful influence. Maybe it was our tribal background, but it never occurred to us to treat any people as less valuable than we.

That does not mean Job was ignorant of the possibility that there are those in the world who meant us harm. Soon after he was accepted into the Council of Elders, he was given the task of overseeing preparations for our protection from marauders. Along with the distribution of justice, security was a primary concern for the Council, which met more and more frequently in our home. There I witnessed the high respect in which Job was increasingly held.

There was no doubt that Uncle Ruel and Job were major powers. That was confirmed for me when Uncle Eliphaz and other leaders would travel long distances on occasion from adjoining nations to engage in consultation meetings. Eventually, Eliphaz, along with Bildad and Zophar, two other sovereigns from neighboring countries, became fast friends as well as colleagues. My Job was the most highly respected of men.

Chapter Seven: Growth, Change, and Crisis

Given the social structure of our household, our small children were rarely taught in the traditional way, by accompanying Job or me as we went about our work, but often our servants brought them along as they did their chores. Our older children, however, did travel out with us, just as I had with my mother-in-law early in my marriage, to learn the ways of supervising and administering our wealth. As for more formal training, the children of the entire household were the focus of care and tutelage equal to that received by our own offspring. For more sophisticated education, one of our best acquisitions was a brilliant slave who became the teacher for the older children.

During the years of marriage, our daily lives departed ever more widely from the practices of our childhood. Some things we never left behind, though—the rule of hospitality, the expectation that our wealth would be shared, the comfort in the presence of a large household, and the awareness of a mutual obligation to protect the members of our tribe and, more broadly, the nation.

As the household grew, many rooms were added to our tent. No longer a shelter only for our family, it was a home for servants as well. But even an enlarged tent eventually became inadequate for our needs. In addition, Uncle Ruel's flock had been growing, as had Job's, so there was no longer space for all of them to graze in the same territory. It was becoming clear, as well, that Job's abode had become a focus not only for the meetings of the Council of Elders, but also for their administrative activities. Therefore, we made plans to move our whole household and our animals to a location some three days' journey away from Uncle Ruel to a building that would fill our needs.

The house we had built was located on a hill overlooking what would, eventually, become a walled city based around our home as a headquarters. I hesitate to say palace. Built of solid rock, there was a huge atrium in the center, shielded by large copper doors, ornamented in bronze. Around that entrance hall in a *U* shape were rooms on the main level and two balconied floors overlooking the atrium. The space on the main level was used primarily for activities of the Council of Elders. The family rooms were located on the top level, with rooms for some of our children and their caretakers on the second level. Some of the rooms on the second level were assigned to our most honored personal servants as well. And there was always ample room for other travelers who might join us in the tradition of hospitality.

Developed at the same time was a city of smaller four-room stone structures to house our servants, including storage rooms, food preparation areas, and space for their personal animals. Eventually, all this was surrounded by city walls, within which there were wells, cisterns, and gardens, both for the planting and harvesting of food and for floral beauty.

When construction was completed, the overall scene was one of luxurious color and texture. The stone buildings varied from mottled gray to pink, almost mauve, appearance. Sometimes, the sun-reflecting textures gleamed so bright they appeared to be almost white, or sometimes luminous yellow. The gardens, planted to produce blossoms throughout the year, provided varieties from red, pink, blue, and white to silver and deep blue. And, of course, there were always different fragrances, depending on the season.

Leaving our marriage tent, much as it had changed from the time our love was first awakened and consummated and from the time of my first birthings, was still a time of mourning for me. Truly, I was awed and overjoyed with the move to our beautiful new location, but I was leaving so much behind. Further, I would have to travel a much greater distance to be with my own parents or even Job's family. The way would be even longer to Adah.

Job and I bore hardly any resemblance to the nomads we had been. Even our clothing was different. Daily, I wore the long, decorated sleeves of a wealthy woman, having no need to do the basic chores of sweeping, milling, baking, water-carrying, cooking, planting, or harvesting. Every day, Job and I were clothed almost as grandly as we had been on our marriage day. One familiar task did remain for me, and that was the pleasure of weaving much of the cloth that we used not only for our family's clothing but for the whole household.

I had very little opportunity to mourn the loss of the tasks that had defined me as a nomad, however, because as Job's responsibilities changed, the daily administration of our wealth fell to me. There would be periods of time when I was away, traveling to supervise the servants caring for our herds or considering the purchase of new pieces of land. I was sent to examine herds of sheep and goats, donkeys, even camels. I never actually did any purchasing without bringing the information home to Job, though I had the right to do so. In whatever we did, we were partners. The dispensation of charity became primarily my business, however. That was a great pleasure for me. The law of hospitality flowed smoothly beyond entertaining visitors to doing well by all who could gain by our generosity, and my mother-in-law had taught me well how to carry it out with tact and appropriateness.

My mother had been right. I did enjoy our "potage" love. She was right, too, that we would have our arguments. There were many, and, because we were both so stubborn, we usually stayed with them until we had found a way to work the problem out. The one that started when I was pregnant for the sixth time was no ordinary one, though. For some reason, I had begun to fret that I missed my old life. I was feeling that something important had slipped away from me.

During that pregnancy, the internal thunderclouds got blacker and blacker. Frequently, I retreated to the privacy of the women's room, sacrificing to Astarte and pleading for her help. Our marriage seemed to be changing in ways that I could not identify, and I felt a hopelessness that made no sense. Everything around me had turned a dull gray, which got drearier as I reviewed my wasted past; I had done nothing to make my life worthwhile. I had given birth to five healthy children, but any fit woman could do that, and other people were doing a fine job of caring for them. I remembered my early lesson to do something useful when things seemed bleak, but even dyeing and weaving gave me no joy. My life was stretching ahead of me, just one long, purposeless repetition of what I had already done, which was giving no satisfaction to me or anyone else.

It seemed that Job had very little need for me, especially now since he was so involved in daily discussion with the group of men who met in our atrium or near the gardens, discussing I knew not what. It was not the Council of Elders, though Uncle Eliphaz often traveled to join them, sojourning in the guest quarters of our home. Job seemed to be experiencing a tension around me that had not been there before, which, of course, added to my distress.

For some reason, I had lost my power to risk an argument. I wanted to ask Job why his body seemed so taut. And why he spent so little time in our bed. I understood his avoiding my body. That had happened on occasion in some of my previous pregnancies. But even then, he had often given me a long and enthusiastic hug when it was least expected. This was different. His presence felt edgy, like the desert storms I had sometimes experienced when no one else seemed to be aware of them.

I thought sometimes that I had caught Job's edginess and made it part of myself. Had not my mother said, "An attack on his body will be an attack on yours, and whenever he is spared, you will be spared. And he will know you in the same way." Maybe this is what she meant. We have truly become one, so we share each other's emotions as well. Perhaps it was Job who was suffering storms inside. Perhaps he was so distant because he did not want to tell me how he was suffering. I should have had the courage to press him to speak.

But maybe he is just tired of me. He could be hesitant to tell me that he longs to take another wife. Perhaps he already has. No, he seems not to have time for that, being so busy with Uncle Eliphaz and the other men.

The whirlwind inside me was something I had never before experienced. It was as if the gates had slammed shut and I was unable to let anything out. What had happened to the Dara who was so good at picking a fight? What had happened to Job and me that we no longer argued? I longed for such a battle, carried to its conclusion until I understood what was happening.

My mother said that she and my father argued because he respected her. Has Job lost his respect for me? Maybe that is why I am feeling so little respect for myself.

Maybe Job is feeling helpless and I am adopting that heavy feeling for myself. Maybe he needs me more than ever to help him through that torment. But why would he, so successful and powerful, be feeling helpless and useless?

I want to ask him. I need to ask him. I am terrified of his answer.

Again I retreated to my own quarters and appealed to Astarte to help me.

One day, as I was trying to go about my business, the storm grew so intolerable that it broke through. The pain ruptured my fear. Hardly realizing what I was doing, I attacked Job verbally when he came home from his daily meeting with those men who seemed to have replaced me as friend and confidant.

"This is more than I can bear, Job. Just what is going on between us? What is happening to our marriage? Have you taken a concubine? No, I think it is even worse; you are giving all your love and devotion to that group of men. I think there is something improper in that."

My voice trembled with more hidden, angry tears than I had any desire to prevent.

"Our life is in no way like it used to be when we were young, or like I expected it to be when we married."

Some sensible part of me knew that was a ridiculous charge, since our lives had so long ago left our traditional roles behind. I can only assume that some old sense of loss was still there.

"You are never in the fields or out with the herds. What are you doing anyway, spending all that time just talking with those men? I am happy to do my share, as my mother used to say, but it is not at all like what I learned to expect in my home. Does it not even bother you that I am making most of the important decisions in our life? Do you not ever long for the old days? Just what is going on here?"

I could see Job flinching, as if I were hitting him. To tell the truth, I wanted to, and that felt good—much better than the helplessness and fear I had been nurturing.

Job came right back at me, anger for anger, and that felt good also.

"So! You are too rich. Your life is too good. You do not have to do the menial chores, and you get to be in control of most of our life, even of our wealth. Do not pretend you dislike being in control. I have known you for a long time, remember? So what are you complaining about?"

"Job, you are avoiding my point."

I am not even sure what the point is. There is something wrong even with his anger. It seems impure, somehow, or shallow, like a fragile cover on a container of fire. Oh, Astarte, help me. I am so frightened. This is not my Job.

It almost seemed it was not rage he was feeling, but anxiety. This would not be the first time that my anger seemed to frighten him, but now there was a different quality.

Then I asked him the question that broke through his discretion.

"What are you doing day after day with those men, anyway? It is not the Council of Elders. You are not making important decisions for our nation. It is almost like you are in love with them. You cannot wait to join them every day. Is it because they treat you like you are so important? I guess I am not the only one who likes to be in control. What are you up to?"

By now, I was trying very hard not to cry. All I wanted was to understand why my tears were straining to erupt and why they would not.

"Dar'," Job's voice turned gentle, even as it yielded to trembling, just as mine had done. "It is not true that you are making the important decisions. Yes, you have the major part in running our daily life and supervising our wealth. Our worldly situation depends largely on what you do. But what I am doing in my discussions with the men is really the most important for us and our position."

"I knew it, Job. It is all about your importance in this world. You really do like being the leader that all the men look up to. That desire has drowned all else in your life that was once important."

"No, Dar', that is not true. It is about God and how He watches over us."

What is he talking about? What does this have to do with the way he has been treating me? Now he is confusing me. Perhaps that is what he wants to do. Is this his way of deflecting the argument? Astarte, help me to understand.

Job's voice was even more gentle and firmer now, as if he were trying to protect me. From what?

"I have come to understand that everything we have is because He has given it to us."

"*He?*" *What is this "he" business? This is making no sense to me.*

"That is what we talk about and study every day. In a way, we have rediscovered a devotion which was abandoned by previous generations of our family."

Our devotion has been to Astarte. How can he say we have abandoned it? I certainly have not.

"Dara, listen to me. This is the most important thing that has ever happened to us—more important than each other, our family, our wealth, our tribe. Please listen. This is why I did not want to tell you. I knew you would be dismayed."

Thank you, Astarte. At least he is finally talking. I am feeling safer, but what is he talking about?

As if he could hear my thoughts, he went on.

"I am talking about the worship of the God of our ancestor, Abraham. You are right. It is that I am in love, not with the men I study with, but with God. The most important thing is to pay homage to Him, and worship Him constantly, offering up to Him all our activities as a tribute. If we do not, His anger can be intense. Truly, because of my concern for you, I have not dedicated my whole self to Him as fully as I should have."

Because of me? What am I being accused of? Now I am not feeling safe at all. Something terrifying is happening.

"I knew you were sensing my stress." He went on. "I should have enlightened you a long time ago. The conflict has been tearing at me, but I did not want to hurt you."

Hurt me? How could this hurt me? If Job has found such happiness with this god, why should it bother me? Why would he not share it with me?

"Job, I can see that the men in this group are dedicated to spending more time with this god than one would ordinarily expect. He must be an important one. Even Uncle Eliphaz travels from afar to be with all of you. So, Job, that is all it is, another god to add to the help we already get from Astarte."

I am relieved. Job has released his secret. Now he can instruct me about this god, and we can go on with our lives, enriched by the knowledge of this other god. Still, there is something in his face, in his eyes, in his whole posture. There is more, I think, and I am terrified of what it may be. Help me, Astarte.

Then he struck me with those terrible words.

"The fact is, this is not just another god. This one insists on being the only God. All the others are false. Like your Astarte, they are just man-made idols, no more than the doll you used to play with when you were little."

The look Job is giving me is more confusing than his words—such sadness and sympathy, even love, infused with a fiery power and determination I have never sensed in him before. Well, perhaps that is not true. That fire may have been part of what was making me uneasy lately.

Now that the door had been thrown open, all that had been hidden within him came out, without hesitation or tact. Perhaps there was no way to be tactful about this.

"Do you hear me? Astarte is a false god. She should not be in our home, and you are offending God and me every time you offer sacrifices to her. I feel guilty and fearful that she is here. I am sorry. I know it hurts you, but she must go."

It was clear that Job had been holding back these words with a great deal of effort. Now that they were released, they came out like a storm that had been contained for too long. He reached out to touch me, thinking he would comfort me, I suppose. But the last thing I wanted right now was to be touched by him.

My breath was gone, but so was the bleakness. In its stead was a torrent of wild anger, confusion, defiance, disbelief …

Astarte, who has protected me through my childhood, through fear and love, through betrothal and marriage, through five birthings—Astarte has to go? Job cannot possibly mean it. He could not be that cruel to me. His love for me would not allow him to do it.

He could not make me. Of course he could not make me. I just would not do it. Now I knew why I was crying, and I did not like that either. I never did like anyone, even Job, to have such power over me. Caught between Job and Astarte? It could not be. Suddenly, I was filled with energy, terrible, undirected energy. I went looking for a broom to sweep the floor. I went to find Astarte. I ran outside. I sat at the loom and got up again. There was no place to stop. There was no comfort. I was furious, scared, alone, powerless, and filled with angry energy. The love was over. Job had abandoned me.

I had to see Adah. I ran around, almost without direction, gathering what I needed for a journey to her. Job kept following me, doing and saying things that made no sense. He himself made no sense to me any more. When he realized what I was up to, he sent for Sophronia, my favorite maidservant, because she was so levelheaded and competent, the way I was before this terrible thing scattered me to the winds.

"Prepare to go with your mistress wherever she goes and serve whatever needs she has."

Poor thing, she was having a hard time pulling herself together when she saw the wildness in my behavior. Job called on two of our menservants to go with us: Timon, who we both knew held me in particular honor, and Sergius, devoted to both Job and me.

None of that really mattered to me. I just had to get away from this place. I had to keep moving. I had to get to Adah. I slipped Astarte into one of my bags and mounted my donkey, ready to leave. It is a good thing Job saw to it that we were provided with supplies, because I was definitely not being practical.

As we four were about to leave, Job held me back. With a look of devotion beyond what I had ever seen from him before, he actually said,

"Dar', I love you. Do what you have to do and come back to me."

I want to believe the love you are declaring and even demonstrating, but how can I?

I wanted that love. I did not want his love. His declaration just added to the turmoil. To love Job, I was being asked to give up my love for Astarte. I wanted to stay angry, though I did embrace him, out of habit, I suppose. I knew Job well enough to recognize that he was afraid I might choose Astarte over him, but I was in no mood to care about that. Then we left.

The journey to Adah was longer and harder than I had remembered. This time, I was pregnant. The heat waves rising from the sand slashed at me, searing through my clothing. The weight of the child inside me bouncing up and down as we rode was a rock ripping at my insides. I wondered if my pregnancy diet, with no salt and fat, might have weakened me. Maybe the hardest part was that the energy fed by my anger and shock eventually abated, and I was left with nothing but sad confusion and bleakness. Job had been right to send servants along with me. I think my grief and dismay over having to choose between Job and Astarte would have been intolerable if I had not had their company, though they were quite subdued, wondering, I suppose, what this sudden frantic trip was all about.

I spent much of the journey holding Astarte tight to my body. She did give me some comfort, but even she could not stop my ruminations.

My life will never be the same. My days of happiness and joy are over. I will never again be able to feel love for Job. This baby will be born to a mother out of whom all emotion has poured. Maybe it will not even succeed in being born. I am an empty shell, living from now on only out of habit.

The desolation of the desert we were passing through was nothing compared to the wasteland inside me. I could feel myself shriveling up in the dryness. I saw no color, either in the flowers of the desert or in myself.

The three-day journey to the west almost stretched into four, given the slow pace I was setting for us. I did feel gratitude to Job for sending the menservants and ample supplies along with us, especially for the tent they set up for protection and rest at night. Sophronia and I lay inside, protected by Sergius and Timon outside the flap. Neither she nor I slept well the first night. She was alert, watching over me as I lived out terrible dreams of being alone in the desert, without water, a dried-up old woman, tossed aside with no one to love or care for me. I was even more exhausted in the morning than I had been when we retired for the night. The exhaustion that slowed me down in the next days' journeys did help me to sleep the following nights. That was a blessing for Sophronia, who certainly needed her rest, but it refreshed me not at all. Each day, I ached and slowed down more.

Chapter Eight: At Home with Adah

Finally arriving at Narmer's camp in the early evening of the third day, I collapsed off my mount into Timon's arms, still clutching Astarte. Adah was, of course, startled to see me. Even more, she was shocked at my condition. Wordless, she spread blankets for me in the women's tent and allowed Timon to carry me in there. Sophronia did not have to be told to bring me water and to wash my face and arms with a cold cloth. That was refreshing, but most of all, I sank deep and comfortably into being home with Adah. Now all I wanted was for Adah to be at my side as I died. I drifted into a deep, healing sleep.

When I woke, I was willing to eat the bowl of potage Adah brought me, and I could sit up and talk with her. I had no desire yet to tell her why I was there, and she did not press me. That is what good friends do for each other—just be present. There was news to focus on, though, and that's how Adah surprised me. She was clearly in the middle stages of pregnancy. Over the years, she had presented Narmer with three babies, two boys and a girl. I had been to visit after each of the three births, even though she had not sent for me to be with her. Each time, I had heard the news when travelers reported it, and I had gone to her immediately. She had always received me kindly.

Mrs. Job

I drifted in and out of sleep, contented and safe with Adah. Sophronia had been through a hard time with me, and I suggested she make herself comfortable, or useful, as it might please her. I was sure Sergius and Timon would have unloaded the supplies Job had sent to share with Narmer and his family, but I asked Sophronia to reassure them that I was recovering safely with my friend.

Thus my old friend and I were left alone to catch up on the details we had been missing about each other. I kept the focus on Adah, whose life was so much like what I had enjoyed as a child. I wondered, though, why she never sent for me when she delivered her babies.

"Oh," she joked, "I just cannot keep up with you. This, apparently, is your sixth pregnancy. I guess you are winning the mother race."

Winning the mother race? What does she mean? I know I have been eager to give Job babies, but I have never thought of it as a race.

"Adah, do you believe we are in a race?"

"Of course I was only kidding. I just hate to bother you when I know how busy you are."

Bother me? I do not want to hear that now, just after my awful struggle with Job.

I found myself remembering the storm I felt when I first brought Adah to see the tent Job was raising for us. Had I been setting up a competition? Bragging without realizing it?

Could it be that I have been in some kind of rivalry with Adah? I do not think so, but is that not what Adah is saying?

The thought was driving me back into empty hopelessness, sickness in the depths of my body.

Have I lost my best friend too? First Astarte and Job, and now Adah? I cannot let myself entertain the thought. Adah and I are too closely woven together.

"Adah, my heart will break if you believe we are rivals, competing with each other to see who has more children. Our friendship is so important to me. You are woven into the very essence of my body. I cannot imagine important things in my life going on without you. Have you changed in your feelings for me?"

"Oh, Dar', of course not. How could we have gone through childhood and so many life events together and now not feel the same deep friendship?"

Doubts had been planted, but I had to shut the door on them. I could tolerate no more pain.

When I emerged from the women's tent the third day and joined the family, it was like being home again. There was her daughter sweeping the tent, her youngest son carding wool, and the flat bread on the plate over the fire. I went with Adah to the well to fetch water, and the next day, we worked together milling the wheat chosen to celebrate my presence. Later, we walked to the market for onions, stopping to smell the aromatic oils and look at the jewelry.

"Your jewelry is finer than most of these pieces," she observed.

I thanked her for noticing. I wished I had left it at home.

In the evening, Narmer and his older son dipped flatbread into the pot with the rest of us and some of their aunts. Sophronia, Sergius, and Timon were with us too. They looked a little uncomfortable at first, not accustomed to participating rather than serving. Here was the law of hospitality in all its warmth. I was home again. My body relaxed a bit, even as I answered questions about my life since we were last together, leaving out the most recent part.

I did not have to ask Adah if she was happy with Narmer. It was obvious in the easy way they interacted. I had not known what fun he was to be with, nurturing so much laughter in all of us. Maybe I was a little jealous of that. Even Sophronia, Sergius, and Timon were totally at ease as they sank into the pleasure of his hospitality.

Adah still did not ask me any questions, but I knew I would have to explain to her why I had come, and in such wretched condition. She did, however, make comment on how I clutched Astarte.

"You still cling to your goddess, I see."

Tears filling my eyes left me no opportunity to hide my mission.

"Adah, I can hardly tell you what has happened. I know I cannot do it calmly, so please forgive me for disrupting the serenity of your family."

Adah leapt to sit beside me with her arm around me. I sank into it, just as I remembered yielding to my mother's care.

Gasping, hesitating, and struggling, I managed to tell her of the impasse that Job had created. This was the first time I had made the effort to state my suffering in words others could understand.

"I cannot fully grasp what I am about to tell you. Most simply, Job has demanded that I cease worshiping Astarte, that I must remove her from our home."

Adah gasped. I did not have to explain why Job's demand was so painful, but I knew I had to try to explain Job's purpose. Even as I suffered the pain and anger, I recognized that his motives were not unkind, though I was far from making sense of them.

"Can you understand that I have to choose between Astarte and Job?"

Adah held me as I sobbed without control, just as Jarna had done long ago when she learned of her betrothal.

"I do not fully understand what Job has demanded of me. He says he has come to accept the jealous god who will not allow us to cling to any others ... something about recovering the god of Abraham who had at one time been our god but been abandoned by our people."

"Are you telling me," Adah asked, "that Job insists that you must worship only this god that he has somehow discovered—or rediscovered? Does he really mean that you must abandon Astarte?

But she has protected you through so many life events. Even this baby you are carrying. What will happen if you lose her care?"

I fell into another fit of weeping, trying to talk even as I cried. It did feel good, though, to know that Adah understood my fears and my pain.

"The terrible thing is that Job has not stopped loving me. I know he has no desire to abandon me. In fact, I am sure he is just as frightened that I may choose Astarte as I am afraid that I will never be able to feel the same about him again. But how can I give up either one of them? It is truly hopeless. Sometimes I wish I could just go back to the nomad I was before Job accomplished such heights."

As soon as I said those last words, I wished I could swallow them back. Would Adah not take them as bragging on my part? But her attention was entirely on me and my suffering.

Mostly our conversation went around in a circle.

"I can see no happy ending to this pain."

Adah did not stop embracing me, but she did pull her body together in determination.

"Dara, the problem is that you must make a choice that will end this dilemma. It must be either Astarte or Job. Now, we must try to help you do that."

I know she is right, but does she have to be so harsh about it? I do not want to sacrifice this pain. At least I am still connected to both Astarte and Job. If I give up the pain, it will be because I have made a choice. And I cannot choose. I love and need them both, though it is only Job who is the aim of my anger. I cannot do this. It is easy for Adah. She is not faced with this agony.

"But Adah, Astarte has not abandoned me. Only Job has done that. And I suppose that is not fair to say either. He did make sure I was well cared for on the journey here, and he did tell me he loves me and wants me to return to him. No, I cannot leave either of them."

Then the sobbing began again. I simply did have to choose, even though I could not.

I knew I had Adah's complete and deep sympathy. She was trying to prevent it, I knew, but she was crying with me. That felt good.

Then she changed the atmosphere somewhat by saying, "Job is not the only one adopting the religion of that one jealous god."

She knows about this god ... more than I do. How can that be?

"I have other friends facing the same thing," she continued. "It seems to be a kind of movement."

Somehow knowing that others had faced this same problem helped me. It seemed a little more like an issue that might be understood.

I am not the only one who has faced this. Then maybe there is something to be learned that can help me.

"As for me," Adah continued, "I have a hard time understanding such a selfish god. Why not share with others? Astarte has never had a problem being comfortable with the fact that there are other gods with their own demands and their own willingness to protect us, as long as we appease her with appropriate sacrifices."

"Adah, you have stated it well. Why should Job and his god be so unyielding, demanding, and selfish? Astarte is truly much more loving and reasonable."

It eased my emotions not at all to grasp that point, but it did move it closer into the category of a problem to be resolved.

Adah continued, "I have observed that some families transfer their devotion to that one god, but in those cases, everyone seems to be comfortable with it, so there is no conflict."

So, some people actually choose to transfer their devotion to this jealous god. There must be something good about it. Of course there must be something good. My Job would not be so adamant about it if this god were not in some way good.

"So, Adah, it seems that part of what is causing my agony is that Job has made a decision without consulting me. Maybe I can understand how that happened. When I think back on it, I can see that it came to him only gradually in his conversations with Uncle Eliphaz and those other men. Once he had made the decision, it was too late to bring me into the discussion. For him, there was no doubt left to talk about."

My sobs had decreased some. Adah had made this more of a problem to be solved. She seemed to have more understanding of Job's god than I did. I guess the similar challenges her friends were experiencing had provided her with more information than I had encountered.

"The problem with the god that Job wants to devote himself to is that he is so masculine. What does he know about what it is like to be a woman? Bleeding? Birthing? Nurturing? What does he know about the way you and I are feeling right now in our pregnancies? How can he understand the love we feel for children who have grown in our own bodies? In fact, how can he know how it is to live under the rule of our fathers and husbands? True, you and I happened to be lucky with the men in our lives, but the fact is, they could be treating us almost any way they wanted to, and we would have no say in the matter."

How wise Adah had become.

Narmer had come in as we were having this discussion. That made me uncomfortable. Somehow, I wanted this just to be between Adah and me. But he would have his say, in what I had come to recognize as his firm but lighthearted way.

"Okay, what you are saying may be true. But do you think it fair to expect us men to be devoted to Astarte? What does she know about being a man? Has she had to take on all the responsibility for keeping a family clothed and fed and sheltered? Has she had to wonder whether his wife's baby is really his? Has she had to be excluded like an outsider when his wife was bleeding, or birthing, or nursing? Can she even understand that we never feel quite so loved by our children as their mother is? Has she had to take all the burden on her shoulders? Has she had to risk her life in battle? Has she had to feel shame for not being as rich as other men? Has she had to resist those urges to make love to a woman who is not your wife?"

Adah's spine was very straight now.

"Wait a minute. You have wanted to make love to some other woman?"

Poor Narmer. Surely he wished he had not said that, but it was interesting to hear a man's point of view. That happened very rarely with the way men's and women's lives were kept separate.

"Of course, Adah. Did you not know that? It is somewhat difficult being faithful to you, especially when your monthly bleeding confines you, or after your birthings. Nor does it help knowing that nothing requires me to be faithful. There is no rule against my taking a concubine, or even another wife. Masculine gods understand that. In fact, they encourage us to spread our seed. I understand that even this god Job has adopted promotes that, as long as we do not use another man's wife. Then we would all have to wonder if the baby is ours."

If what he was saying was true, then it was an honor to Adah that she was his only wife. I think she was beginning to feel complimented. I know I was as I thought of Job's faithfulness. And I thought of poor Jarna, married to that old man who already had other wives.

My depression and anxiety abated somewhat as this conversation went on. I loved Narmer's humor, and I loved having such an open discussion with a man other than Job or my father. I was also fashioning a solution. Maybe I could keep my devotion to Astarte, but secretly, so it would cause no pain for Job. That way, we could have both masculine and feminine protection. It occurred to me, too, that Narmer was right. Astarte was not devoted to Job's welfare. I began to feel sympathy for Job, left in the dark, so to speak, with my devotion to Astarte. It truly had never occurred to me to make sacrifices for Job's welfare. Two gods, one masculine and one feminine. It was a solution worth thinking about. Astarte in the women's room where she could attend to us without causing trouble for Job.

Being with Adah and Narmer had me feeling a bit nostalgic. Funny how the deeply familiar can feel so much better than the wealth I had hardly noticed I was enjoying. At the same time, I was missing my home and family, especially my children. My anger with Job was beginning to fade into a new understanding of his need for a god of his own.

With Narmer's help, I had developed a new appreciation for the turmoil Job must have been experiencing as he struggled to bring this god of Abraham into his life without bringing conflict to his own family. I was still discomfited, however, with the fact that he could not fully worship this god to his satisfaction unless I joined him. It made no sense to me that his god demanded to be the only one. Why could he not be like the other gods we knew and just fight to keep his place with all of them?

I sojourned a few more days with Adah, enjoying the warmth of her welcome and the familiarity of her home. But I was beginning to be aware how much I yearned to return to Job and let him know that I wanted to please him. But it was not yet clear to me just how I wanted to resolve this. The urge to see Uncle Ruel began to grow in me. It would mean a lengthy detour on the route home, but I had such love and respect for him.

The truth is, I did not want to return home yet. The turmoil inside me was far from subsiding. I was sure he would be able to help me resolve this. Besides, his Uncle Eliphaz was apparently a big influence on Job's convictions. Maybe Uncle Ruel could explain Eliphaz to me.

So it was that I took leave of Adah. First, I made her promise that she would come when I birthed my child, and that she would send for me when hers was newborn. We sealed the promises with a long hug. We loved each other. She and Narmer sent us on our way with an ample supply of food and water, pleased, I think, that they could be generous to us. I tucked Astarte into my travel bag and enjoyed the feeling of being stronger and refreshed as we rode southeast toward Uncle Ruel.

Chapter Nine: The Wisdom of Elders

Now that I had decided to pay this visit, I could hardly wait to see Uncle Ruel, just as I had felt when I was a child. Funny how he was still "Uncle Ruel" to me, even though he was my father-in-law. It was not so with Beta, my mother-in-law. I admired her, for she was a fine woman who had taught me a great deal and made many kind gestures, especially in her offerings to Astarte, but I did not feel the intense warmth for her that I did for Uncle Ruel. I knew she would be present for the birth of this child I was carrying, or at least soon after the birth, but she no longer received my babies when they were delivered. That usually fell now to Sophronia. Things changed when we could afford servants. My mother still supported my back, though, assuming she made the journey soon enough to be there while I was still laboring. It pleased her to be part of the process.

The trip from Adah to Uncle Ruel was somewhat more comfortable. My baby was still a heaving, jolting rock inside me, and the heat still slapped against me in searing waves, but my eyes and ears were open to the world around me. As we rode past it, I felt the cool comfort of a watering hole surrounded by sheep and goats refreshing themselves along with their shepherd. The calm pinkish-brown and black of the animals against the gray and silver of the ground, the blue of the water, and the cool shade cast by the two sycamore trees washed me in serenity even as a part of me struggled with my pain. I knew that traveling to Uncle Ruel would help me.

Sophronia, Timon, and Sergius were clearly reassured by the improvement in my condition. Timon even pulled out his reed flute and began playing soothing music which led Sophronia and Sergius to join in song. After a while, I did too. It was as if there were two layers of feeling going on inside me. At the top was a kind of relaxed joy in this sharing and nostalgia. Underneath was a sandstorm of doubt and confusion. And how I missed Job! Hardly thinking of what I was doing, I removed Astarte from her case and pressed her to my breast.

It occurred to me that Uncle Ruel might not be home. Like Job, he traveled often on the business of the Council of Elders. I decided I would wait for him if he were not there. The need to see him had become more than a strong desire; it seemed like my very life depended on it.

Arriving at Uncle Ruel's was such a different experience from visiting Adah. It was not a tent we approached, but the doorway to a house that was much like ours, though a bit smaller. Like ours, the entrance revealed an open courtyard in the center, around which, in a *U* shape, were rooms. The lower rooms were for the household servants, while the family resided in the balconied upper rooms. It was not just the structure that was different from Adah's tent. Being received by a servant was nowhere near as warm as Adah's very personal greeting. The warmth came, however, when Uncle Ruel gave me his wonderful hug. Like my father, he was aging a little, but he still had his handsome power. I was so relieved to find him at home.

Once I had washed and was lounging with the family around the lavishly appointed meal table, I plunged into the story of my dilemma. Sophronia and the menservants were being well cared for in the servants' quarters, and I felt free to discuss these issues. My mother-in-law just listened, though it was clear she understood my distress at the threat of losing Astarte. Uncle Ruel, however, seemed not at all surprised by my story. In fact, I think he was not at all surprised to see me.

"I know," he said, "this is a far cry from what you knew as a child. Everything about your life with my son is different from the nomadic life you lived when you were young. I can understand how important it is for you to hold on to something as familiar as Astarte." He framed it so well. I was relieved that he understood, but I wanted to be sure he comprehended the conflict I was suffering between my love for Job and my adoration of Astarte. Even as I tried to make that clear to him, however, I heard him connect Astarte to my nostalgia for my early years. Was that what Astarte meant to me?

I appreciated the respect he gave me. He could just as well have ordered me to adopt Job's god. Job had, after all, the authority over me. But he seemed instead to be anxious to help me understand the value of this deity. I realized as we talked that he himself had accepted that god of Abraham. He seemed firm in his convictions, but he did not try to lecture me. Instead he asked me about my adoration of Astarte. He asked me how often I sacrificed to her. Or when did she help me? My answer required a lot of thought.

"I certainly did cling to her when I left home this time, so agitated in my despair. And I always turn to her when I am birthing a child. After all, she is a female. She understands. In fact, I have felt her loving and comforting touch when I was enduring the pain of childbirth."

I reported to him and my mother-in-law my conversation with Adah and Narmer about the difference between a feminine and a masculine god.

"She was with me when I got betrothed and when I got married. In fact, I call on her whenever there is some kind of major change or crisis in my life."

"And where is she now?" Uncle Ruel asked.

I told him I had set her near my bed in the room they had given me. I found myself longing to fetch her. I wondered where he was going with this, especially when I saw a look on my mother-in-law's face that told me she had been through this discussion.

"So tell me, what is she doing while she is placed by your bed?"

I had the feeling I was about to get trapped, but I had to say, "Nothing. She is just waiting."

Then he paused. In the long silence, I began to understand that she was not always there for me, but only when I called on her. But how, I wondered, was that different from any other deity, waiting to be asked for what we wanted, and ready to be angry if we appealed to any other deity to the neglect of themselves. This conversation was not helping. Now I had to be afraid that Astarte would be angry with me if I let Job's god into my life. She would not be good to me the next time I asked.

"The God that Job and I have come to worship is different, Dar'. He is always there. He does not wait for us to call on Him, but watches over us and takes care of us even when we are not aware of His presence. In fact, that loving and comforting touch you felt in the pangs of childbirth was the God of Abraham, who blesses us even when we don't ask."

It wasn't Astarte who comforted me? That was more than I wanted to believe. But somehow, I had to admit that this god was beginning to feel like my father and Job and Uncle Ruel all rolled into one. Maybe he was like a good father or uncle.

"But what does he know about women's things, like giving birth or loving like a mother?"

"Oh Dar', He has given birth to the whole world, to all of us. Imagine how that labor felt, and the watching over everyone at all times."

I told Uncle Ruel that I suspected giving birth to the world did not feel much like giving birth to a human baby. His argument helped me only a little. But he was persistent. He told me that another important thing about this god of Abraham and giving birth to us was that he created us in his own image. I took issue with that, too. Ruel did, after all, say "his" image.

"That is just a manner of speech," he said. "Of course that includes females as well."

This seemed a little strange to me.

"Then where can I go to see him to know what this male/female god looks like?" I asked.

Uncle Ruel told me I could not see him.

"In fact, God does not like it if anyone tries to see Him or make a statue of Him. You can only feel Him, just to be aware of His presence."

"Then how do you know any of what you have told me is true? Does Uncle Eliphaz have something to do with it?" There, I had expressed my suspicions.

"Well, yes, he does. He was the first to bring us the message. Actually, he reminded us of a message that has been with us all along, but our people have tended to forget it. Eliphaz restored a belief we should never have neglected. If you could see how excited he is about this, and how committed he is to God, you would be convinced too. His opinion is pretty powerful considering what a wise and respected elder he is."

This was feeling a little insane to me, and even more insane when I realized my mother-in-law had come to believe it too. I wondered—was she just giving in to Uncle Ruel's demand? I did not want to discuss it any more. I certainly had not resolved my dilemma, but I did have many questions and much to think about.

We changed the conversation to stories of how my children were growing and how my pregnancy was developing. Of course it was now my mother-in-law who was most enthusiastically involved. Uncle Ruel just stayed quiet and listened. I could tell he had decided to give me time to think about what had been said. It was clear, however, that he was hoping to talk me into accepting this god who shares space with no others. A big part of me wished I could do that. It would make it easy to be happy with Job again.

But even if I began to believe, I was never one to yield easily in an argument or to admit that someone else was right. I had a lot to think about as I retired for the night on the soft mattress in the room I had all to myself. I was lonely, so I took Astarte into the bed with me and begged her to help me. Nothing happened. I pulled her closer to me, but I did not feel the comfort I had felt when I first left home, clinging to her all the way. Was she angry with me? I realized that I was fingering the gold Astarte on the chain that Uncle Ruel had given me as a betrothal gift. It had become a common practice to which I gave no thought. No blessing flowed from the act. Had Astarte just vanished without a farewell?

A god who was always with me. One I would not have to tuck away in a bag, or pull out again in a crisis? I liked the idea. I wished I could believe. I had a question for Uncle Ruel the next day.

"What does your new god like in the way of sacrifice?"

"He likes burnt offerings, ra', of sheep or goats or perhaps another animal, but never humans."

It seemed to me that he was not so different from Astarte, then. She liked sacrifices too.

He had no good reply for that one, except to acknowledge that it was true.

"But," he said, "Astarte and God are different in some pretty important ways. First of all, Astarte is a household god. She serves only the household that accepts her as their personal deity, and then you cannot always be sure she will do as you ask. Think about it. Does she?"

I thought about the birth of my first child. How I had begged Astarte to spare me pain, but in truth, the cramps were very intense. Uncle Ruel pointed out that Astarte acted on whim. Sometimes she would care for us, and other times, she would just ignore us. When you come right down to it, she is sometimes unfair in her treatment of us.

"Job's God and mine, on the other hand, is always just. He understands that people are not perfect, but when we work to obey His laws and avoid major sins, He treats us fairly."

Uncle Ruel admitted that the God of Abraham, his God and Job's, does ask a lot of us. He does expect us to worship Him regularly, not just when we need something, but the justice he gives us in return makes it all worthwhile.

"So," I wondered, "if I pray to Job's god when I am about to deliver this baby, can I be sure I will suffer no pain?"

"That is not the way it works with God," he told me. "It is in the nature of human birthing that there will be pain, just as the men will have to work hard to supply food and shelter for the family."

Now I thought of Narmer's complaints about the requirements of being a man.

And I thought of Jarna and her betrothal to the older man who already had several wives. Was Job's god being just? Would Jarna have been better off if she had believed in Job's god? Uncle Ruel acknowledged that he could not pretend to know the answer to that.

"I only know it is not the kind of day-to-day thing that God is involved in. He has already created us with what we need to handle that. It is in the big things that His justice shows most clearly. No major harm will come to those who worship Him. And that takes us back to the sacrifices. Their purpose is to show God that you believe in Him and hope He will overlook any sins you may have committed. The idea is to make it clear that we understand that He is the all-powerful only God, and He is just."

Fairness was always a big thing with me. I could get very upset when things happened that were not just. Maybe I could like this god of fairness. It certainly would make Job happy. This god seemed pretty strong, and I liked that he felt like Uncle Ruel and Job and my father all rolled into one. But I would not lie about my convictions, either to Job or to myself, so I would have to think about it. If he was that powerful, it was really hard to believe that he was part female.

Uncle Ruel and my mother-in-law left me alone with my thoughts. I stayed with them for another three days, letting myself feel the strength of their understanding and protection. I hardly noticed that I left Astarte standing where I had put her when I woke up after the first night at their home.

All this thinking about men who took care of me led me to longing for my father. Suddenly I felt that I must see my parents, so I took leave of my parents-in-law and headed northeast toward my old home.

I realized as we traveled that my emotions were not so divided as they had been on my way to Uncle Ruel's. I could not have explained why, but I knew deep down that everything would work out well, though I did not know how it could happen. It was as if I were coming alive again after a long sojourn on the threshold of death. Now I noticed familiar things in the desert, evoking nostalgic appreciation for my childhood home. There was a herd of camels, and fields of silver blossoms, and then suddenly the caves where Adah and I had enjoyed our winters near each other. I had heard people talk about being filled with emotion. Now I knew what they meant—the pleasant pain of a swelling heart.

Reminiscences flooded in as I approached my parents' settlement. I guess I was in the mood to reach deep into myself, because truthfully, not much was different for me to notice in their home. I had been visiting them often, frequently bringing their grandchildren to see them. I suppose they were aging, but I did not notice it happening. They had not changed their way of living very much either, though they could have. My father's herds had multiplied over the years. That is what happens when you have good herds in the first place and care for them well. Multiplying is what they do. But my parents liked the way they lived in the midst of the tribe. My father's position was as honored as Uncle Ruel's, and I know he was proud of that. But aside from the beautiful rugs on the floor of the tent, more beautiful serving vessels, and a change of diet that included more costly foods, their life was as I had left it when I rode off on my wedding day. I felt comfortably at home, just as I had at Adah's.

This was not just an ordinary visit, though, and over our evening potage, I easily opened the discussion. I told them the whole story of Job's demands, my visits to Adah and to Uncle Ruel, and what I had learned in the process. My presentation was nowhere near as emotional as it had been on my other two visits. I was already feeling much calmer and hopeful that I was finding a resolution to the Astarte issue.

On my way to them, I had practiced saying to myself, "This god is the only god. This god is the god of Job and Eliphaz and Uncle Ruel. Adah and Narmer have heard of this god, and they think it is acceptable that he is a masculine god. And Uncle Ruel thinks that females are created in this god's image too."

I had repeated over and over again, "Job's god is the only god; I can worship Job's god only," just to get a feel for it.

Would I be able to say it honestly? Would I be true to myself and honest with Job if I told him on my return that I had accepted his god? It did not feel completely right to me.

I needed to hear my parents' reactions, especially my mother's. After all, she was the one who had taught me to revere Astarte.

My father's response was immediate: "Of course you will adopt Job's god. Job is the head of the family."

I almost laughed; his response was so typical of the role of the commanding male and so unlike my father, who had always examined and discussed every major issue with my mother, even if it was true that the final authority was his.

My mother was smiling too as she told me that they also had been hearing about this movement to worship only that one god. In fact, they had been discussing it.

"I am happy to say that your father so far is satisfied with my worship of Astarte, so I am not faced with your problem. I will understand, though, if you decide to accept Job's god."

Until she said that, I had not realized that my body had continued to be tense even as I approached the home of my parents. Now I felt a massage of calm rolling through me. Even my baby seemed to quiet down inside me. We went on to enjoy the hospitality of my childhood home, sharing it with Sophronia, Sergius, and Timon. They seemed more comfortable than they were at first at Adah's when they were expected to eat and sleep with the family. I think maybe they were feeling easier too, seeing my body become less taut.

That night, my mother offered me her household Astarte, the one with whom I had grown up, to guard my sleep. I accepted; then I had two Astartes by my side. As I lay there before drifting off, I realized that they were both statues. The real Astarte must also be invisible like Job's god. These statues were just representations of her.

I dreamt that night—a lovely dream. I saw Job's god, a mixture of Job and my father and Uncle Ruel, embracing Astarte, and she returned the embrace. As if in marriage, she was becoming one with Job's god. Together, they were one god. I could go home happy to Job. My problem was solved. Maybe the joining of the god of Abraham and Astarte would not bear truth for other people, but for me, it was a deep and moving reality. The feeling was still there in the morning. Astarte had melded into Job's god. I could have my masculine and feminine god and the love of my husband. Ecstasy, relief, calm satisfaction, indescribable feelings of comfort—all were mine.

We stayed with my family four more days, during which I recited over and over to myself, "Job's god is the only god."

It became easier and easier. Every once in a while I told myself, "Job does not have to know I see his god embracing Astarte."

While I was there, I became increasingly aware that the child inside me was hoping to be birthed soon. I warned my mother that I might be sending for her as soon as I got home.

Before I left, I wove a blanket like the one my mother had made for my doll years earlier. I lay my Astarte in straw and said good-bye to her. I thanked her for being the wonderful companion who watched over me, wrapped her in her blanket, and placed her carefully in a woven box my mother provided for me. As a parting gift to her, I laid the gold betrothal chain around her neck, crying as I parted with the touch of Uncle Ruel. I told her I knew she had become the feminine part of Job's god. When I got home, I would put my doll in there with her and store them both in a far corner of the women's room. I was at peace and eager at the same time to get home to Job and my children.

Chapter Ten: Piety and Twilight

"Job's god is my god. Job's god is the only god. There is only one god. Job's god is the one god."

Now I thought the journey would never end. Excitement was pumping through my body. My baby was feeling it too. I wanted to be home. I wanted to be with Job. I wanted to see my children. I wanted to tell Job the good news: "Your god is my god."

He was there when I arrived. Our embrace proved that a "figs-and-pomegranates-and-special-cheeses" love can supplant "potage love," even after all these years, with a hug that wraps itself around a baby about to be born.

But the embrace did not last long. Our baby was easing her way out with determination and haste.

"Job, I want you to receive this baby."

I did not give him the opportunity to resist. There was no time for that. I led him into our room and, almost completely without pain, delivered a beautiful baby girl into his hands. I was sure her birth was a message from Job's god. Narmer had complained that men were excluded from birthing. Now my Job had been part of it. I felt it was a special gift to him from me and from his god. Job named her Nefer, which means "beautiful." Throughout her life, he never stopped adoring her in a special way.

Sophronia arrived with the necessary linens and oils to take over care of the baby, and Job did not get the doubtful pleasure of witnessing the afterbirth.

I went through the cleansing ritual Job told me was required by his god and spent the purifying time in seclusion, longer because I had given birth to a girl. The truth is, I enjoyed the period of peace and quiet. Left alone, I thanked Job's god repeatedly. After a while, I realized I was no longer saying, "Job's god," but simply, "God." I did not think God minded that I saw Astarte in his embrace, but I did not tell Job.

When it was time, I sent for my parents and Adah and Narmer and Uncle Ruel and my mother-in-law, and everyone else who wanted to celebrate with us. Unfortunately, Adah was not able to come, because of her pregnancy, I assumed. I missed her, but otherwise, I was surrounded by all my loved ones. This time, we feasted on a fatted calf Job had sacrificed to our God.

I guess Job had begun to feel relieved as soon as he told me about his jealous God. While I was gone, he had his servants, under his careful supervision, begin erecting a massive sacrificial altar. It stood above even our home, at the highest pinnacle of the hill, overlooking our city below. A solid base of earth and stone had been formed, with steps of rock leading to a terrace on which a frame of acacia wood was built. Within the frame were heaps of rock supporting a constant fire maintained by burning oils, regularly replenished by a slave assigned specifically to that duty. Occasionally, ashes were removed and piled outside the altar, still sacred as offerings to God. The altar had a façade of gold leaf, mingled with silver and bronze, and sprinkled with precious carnelian of blood red, orange, peach, and pomegranate rose, along with agate combinations of black, brown, and milky white. Those gems on my wedding sleeves had been beautiful. On Job's altar, they recreated heaven on its brightest days, almost blindingly reflecting the intensity of the sun. God was present there in all His majesty.

In creating the terraced access to the altar, Job had our cultivated flower gardens expanded to the hillock leading to it. They were new growth which would explode in intense blues, reds, yellows, and oranges as they matured, just as our devotion to God would magnify.

My husband had also made arrangements for the men of the household to be circumcised. He had waited for me to come back so I would not be shocked that he had done it. The truth is, I was pretty horrified that God required it. Job and our sons had their foreskins removed first, and Job offered them up in sacrifice. I confess, I was angry with God, or maybe with Job, for putting himself and our sons through such anguish.

I told Job, as he and our boys lay around suffering, how angry I was with God, and how confused and guilty I was feeling because of it. He assured me it was acceptable to be angry with God. It showed how much faith I had developed that I could be outraged without fearing He would abandon us. Again I thought of the way I felt with Job and Uncle Ruel and my father, the assurance I had that they would love me and care for me no matter what.

I was seeing the advantage of being a woman, however, when all the other men of the household had to go through the same procedure. Once again, Job offered up the foreskins in sacrifice to God. In fact, Job was sacrificing to God almost every day. He seemed overjoyed that he could finally be so public with his belief. It was also important to him to share the blessings of his devotion with all the inhabitants of the city. As time passed, he would occasionally sacrifice sufficient animals to have a major feast for the entire community.

Nefer was healthy and calm, none the worse for the terrible journey she had taken with me in my search for Job's faith. I felt particularly close to this little one after what we had been through together and nursed her for a full four months before yielding her to the wet nurse. I did not want to give up the thrill of her little mouth drawing on my breast, but I had to think of becoming pregnant again to enlarge our family further.

I began hoping for word from Adah that her time had come. I would have loved to be with her in the birthing. Finally I could wait no longer, so I sent Servius to her. I told him to take with him whomever he needed, and I sent fifty goats and a pair of donkeys as a gift—a thank-you gesture for the help Adah and Narmer had given me on my last distraught visit. Mostly, my mission for Servius was to bring back word of Adah's newborn.

Servius returned with the goats and the donkeys and word that Adah had indeed borne a healthy baby boy about a month ago.

"They thanked you for the gift but refused to accept it, asking me to deliver the message that they had no need for charity."

What have I done to bring this pain upon myself? Once again, Adah has given birth without including me in the joy. And she has refused to accept my gifts. What has happened to our deep friendship? Have I offended her? Of course I have. Obviously that's why they have rejected my gifts. But how have I offended? Maybe I should not have imposed myself on her and Narmer when I was so upset about Job's God.

I just cannot bear the loss of Adah. I've got to see her and Narmer to explain the gifts I sent. I meant them as an offering in exchange for the life-saving gift of hospitality and counsel they gave me in my time of need. Maybe they do not understand that they saved my life. Maybe I have not really understood it until now. I must journey to Adah's. I cannot accept this without explaining myself and understanding what she has done.

Job blessed my journey and blessed Sophronia and Servius on their journey to accompany me. But he refused to allow me to take the gifts back to Adah and Narmer. He said he did not want to humiliate them. With his example, I was beginning to understand the discomfort Adah and Narmer felt as our riches seemed to separate our two families. When I visited them, I was returning to the familiar. When Adah thought of coming to me, it must have seemed like a journey into another world, one where she may have felt she did not belong.

Just before we left, I changed my clothes. Now it did not seem right to be wearing my usual undergarment with intricately woven full sleeves. I changed into a sleeveless ankle-length linen tunic with a brown sash and a deep brown robe over it, more like our tribe's daily wear. I removed much of my jewelry too. My understanding had grown that my wealth was offensive, or at least uncomfortable, for Adah, and that trying to share it only made it more distasteful.

As the three of us rode off together, I knew Job was planning to go immediately to offer a burnt sacrifice to God. It would be his way of protecting us. And we did have a good journey together as Sophronia and I rode ahead, with Servius riding somewhat behind as if to watch over us, or perhaps even to avoid intruding on our conversation. Sophronia and I had become closer than mistress and servant through all the emotional hazards we had shared. Having enthusiastically adopted Job's God after our last trip together, she was ready to live the fact that we were equal in His eyes. So it was that we spent the trip talking about Timon. "Talking" is probably not a good word for it. I spent my time listening to her adoration for the man. "If he and I had parents in this country, I would be asking them to arrange our marriage."

With all our charity for others, I had been oblivious to the pain many of our servants must have felt, having been torn from their own tribes in distant countries and brought to us to serve. As we rode our separate mounts, it was not possible for me to reach out and embrace her, but I let her know that was what I was doing emotionally.

"If you and Timon accept it, Sophronia, Job and I will arrange your marriage."

I was afraid her joy would cause her to dismount and kneel in thanks. I would have sickened at the sight of that humiliation. Sophronia was my friend.

When Adah saw us riding into her camp, her expression was strange. She seemed to be happy to see us, and at the same time, she looked behind us suspiciously, as if she feared we had brought back the gift of goats and donkeys. She seemed relieved when we unloaded only the acceptable foods one would expect a visitor to bring. It had also become a kind of tradition that I brought her a new woven blanket for each baby, and she was as happy to accept it this time as she had been in the past. Again she pointed out that it had meaning because it was a gift of my own making.

Bringing up the issue of the intended purpose of the rejected gifts was not easy. That waited for an opening the second day of our visit. On the first evening, sitting cross-legged around the fire pit and enjoying the potage with the flat bread, I again found myself nostalgic for the familiar, and when Adah suckled her beautiful new baby, my own breasts swelled with aching yearning to put my own little one to my bosom. I guess it would not be right to say I was jealous, but I was, in a sense, grieving for a past that would never return.

Adah and Narmer did accept my explanation for the rejected gifts. They understood that I was deeply grateful for the care they had shown me beyond all requirements of hospitality. But they did not accept that I had to display my gratitude so lavishly. They were my friends, and that is what friends do, they told me. I felt somehow chastised. But when I asked for it, I received no good explanation for the fact that Adah never sent for me when her babies were born. What she told me was that she was too busy to find someone to fetch me. It was easier for me because I was surrounded by servants, she said. I knew that had not been true when my first babies were born, but it felt too risky to point that out, so I let the conversation come to an end.

We stayed two days with my oldest and dearest friend. Sophronia seemed to enjoy listening to our reminiscences and joined enthusiastically in our laughter as we recalled some of the mischief we had enjoyed. It was clear, however, once we were heading home, that she could hardly contain her eagerness to see Timon. I longed a little for the times when Job and I were first married and my days were filled with such constant "figs-and-pomegranates-and-special-cheeses" love. I determined to set Job and myself to work arranging a wonderful wedding for these two favorite servants.

Timon and Sophronia were married in a beautiful ceremony, in some ways like the one Job and I had enjoyed. The tribal headdress was not appropriate, since their community was primarily our large household, but we were able to supply a substantial dowry. In that function, as in all the others around the wedding day, Job and I stood in as parents. The feast was as lavish as their clothes were fine. In fact, no effort was spared to make the celebration of their union worthy of royalty, which they almost were, being so closely connected to Job.

Over the years, Sophronia gave birth to many beautiful children who, as they grew older, were taught by the same tutors from whom our children learned.

Things do have a way of falling into place. Job's responsibilities as a leader were multiplying, as was the number of our servants. He was now completely devoted to the daily teaching and study of the Holy Writings when he was not involved in major functions for the Council of Elders. Sophronia and Timon became honored officers trusted with the primary care of our wealth. Servius also became a major functionary, having responsibility for carrying out my plans for charitable distribution of our wealth. In that role, he traveled widely, surveying the needs of our community.

As for me, my function as a wife was vastly different now from what it had been in the beginning, or what I had imagined when I was living in my parents' home. When I was not overseeing the needs of the household and, indeed, of our city, I was occasionally free to spend time with my growing children and travel to be with my parents. My visits to Adah continued to be regular, though I was not able to get her to sojourn with me—not even when I gave birth. Much to my satisfaction, I found time to spend dyeing and weaving, mostly for clothing for our household, but sometimes for sale or barter with traveling merchants. It was not that I needed additional riches, but it was satisfying to know my creations were appreciated.

Job never failed to honor God with sacrifices of the purest of our flock, especially on important occasions. He never failed, either, to show his love for me. True, it was mostly "potage" love, inspired only occasionally by the old excitement. By the time I was twenty-nine years old, I had given birth to ten healthy children, the last two of whom were daughters. In all, our family was blessed with seven sons and three daughters. My birthing was done.

Both Job and I were happy with the size of our family, and in the tradition of our God, I had the final say about when we would demonstrate our love for each other. With God's blessing, we were able to enjoy each other as husband and wife while avoiding further pregnancies. Nothing was lacking in our lives: joy in our family; abundant wealth; wide opportunities to practice hospitality and charity; esteem beyond what we had ever anticipated; confidence in God's loving care for us; and the pleasure of devoted friends and servants. Even our parents were granted long and healthy lives. It was clear that God was rewarding Job richly for his devotion.

Our two youngest daughters had enjoyed betrothal ceremonies which pleased both them and us. As they approached womanhood, they led lives somewhat similar to what mine had been, and yet different. Each one had a best friendship, just as I had with Adah, but the tribal atmosphere was not at all the same. Our daughters never swept the floor of a tent or even lived in one. When they helped to mill flour, it was not a necessity but a fun thing to do when they were spending time with the servants. They took their meals reclined around our elaborate table with its bronze decorations, not sitting cross-legged around the family pot. They never had the grown-up feeling I had enjoyed of fetching water from the well for the family. A trip to the market was a quick walk in the city, not the expedition Adah and I had enjoyed.

But they giggled with their friends, played at being married and having children, and admired silks, jewelry, and precious oils, which they were not often allowed to buy. Their lessons continued in formal sittings with their teacher, unlike the practical following-along that trained Adah and me. Visits from important members of the Council of Elders were no more exciting than daily chores for them.

And they were given daily chores. We would have failed in their upbringing if we had not required that they be useful wherever they could. I was particularly pleased with the passion they each brought to carding, dyeing, spinning, and weaving. They were ready to maintain the family reputation.

Life was different for Job and me and our family from the tribal atmosphere in which we had grown up. Almost without realizing it, we had arrived at a pinnacle of life that neither of us had anticipated, planned for, or even dreamed of. It just seemed to happen. Our married children had established their own households, some in our city and others, like Primus, at some distance from us. All were busy with their own growing families. That is what we were discussing one day as we sat together enjoying the beauty of our home, the land around us, and the city below.

Our married children and their families were all at the home of Primus, feasting together as they did once each year. We had even allowed our two youngest daughters to travel in the company of a servant to join them in their festivities. This was a particularly important event, not only because all our offspring would be together, but also because we rejoiced in the fact that they all got on so well with each other. God had truly blessed us in the health and solidarity of our family.

Job, praying for the safety of our whole family, especially that they would remain pious and faithful to God's commandments while they were together, had asked me to arrange that one of the healthiest and fattest calves be set aside for the sacrifice he would make when they all came to us after the celebrating was over. That is what he always did. Being the master of the household, indeed of his whole family, no matter how scattered, it was his responsibility to keep them all practicing the faith with devotion. Ever mindful that it is easy to stray, and especially that his oldest children had not been brought up in the laws of the faith from the beginning, he feared they might offend God in their hearts, or even carelessly commit outright sin.

We were in the early evening of our lives, enjoying the blessings God had bestowed on us, appreciating how much we owed Him in the way of devotion. In fact, we were just feeling calm, good, and happy as we quietly celebrated our lives together. Seated in the silver-hued, gold-leaf-decorated carved acacia wood chairs our servants had placed for us on the courtyard in front of our home, we looked out over our city, warmed in our hearts and souls by the silver light glistening off the acacia trees, the variegated greens of the sycamores, and the pinks, yellows, reds, and blues of our massive cultivated gardens, rising on the steep terraced hillock approaching our home and the gleaming altar above it. Even our purple garments added to the display and to the awareness of God's gift to us of great good fortune.

Below us in the city moved the occasional group of camels inside our city wall, and the constant comings and goings of our servants, their families, and their animals, wandering through the lush display of their own private gardens. Everyone in the city had, over time, adopted our God as their own, perhaps because they witnessed the blessings Job and I received, perhaps because they recognized themselves as fortunate, or perhaps because worship of our God just felt good to them. Whatever the reason, the men were dedicated enough to have submitted to the required circumcision, and all were devoted to following the laws as Job taught them.

We were alone together as we had been on the first day after our wedding celebrants had left us, but certainly not lonely as we viewed the fruits of our lives together. The sun was in its quiet season, surrounding us with warmth, but calmly, without the searing waves of truly hot summer. I thought of the contrast between this day and those of my frantic journey with Nefer in my belly, in search of Job's God. What a mistake I might have made had I not accepted our God. I reached out to touch Job and felt a sweet twinge of figs and pomegranates.

Chapter Eleven: The Trials

In an instant, it was over. It began when the action in the city below us turned into a rustle of confused activity, calling our attention to our servant Zosimus in the distance, staggering toward us. By the time he reached us and fell at our feet, we knew the peaceful loveliness of our day was over.

"Master, the Sabeans attacked us while the oxen were plowing and the donkeys were grazing. They took them all and killed all the servants tending them. They left only me alive to come and tell you." Shuddering almost beyond control, my body reproduced my awful childhood fears of cruel and destructive people. But now they were real.

I have to make my body firm. So many deaths. We must arrange for the burials. Who will console their families? How will we ever make up for the loss of all these animals?

I was about to tell Zosimus to go refresh himself in whatever way he required when the wild atmosphere below us drew our eyes to our servant Tacitus running and falling in a desperate effort to reach us. He fell down beside Zosimus, trembling uncontrollably, able only to scream silently at first.

I glanced at Job, ashen and silent as I was. I was not shuddering now, nor was my body firm. I was without feeling even as I smothered more pain than had ever before filled me. Then Tacitus spoke.

"Lightning struck from the sky and burned up all the sheep and the shepherd boys. I am the only one who lived through it, and I rushed to tell you."

I could not move. I was a stone monument affixed to my seat. Neither Job nor I could speak to tell these poor servants to care for themselves. I tried to reassure myself.

We were happy in our early years, without our great wealth. We can survive this loss. We are still alive. Our family is still alive. I must not think of myself, for I have to attend to the poor people whose loved ones died in these attacks. All those lives lost. And only a few moments earlier, we had been celebrating our lives so calmly. We were so sure we lived under the protection of God. Where is God now?

My thoughts were ripped away when the scene below us seemed to undulate in random confusion like a huge slithering snake and we saw a third servant weaving, falling, and crawling his way up to us like an agonized spirit hardly connected to his own body. The day became a dream, a nightmare. The trees and flowers and camels sank into the earth. The families we had been watching vanished. Everything around us had disappeared into emptiness, except for this servant approaching the fetid remains of our lives. Falling on top of the other two messengers, he managed to groan, "Chaldeans have attacked. They took the camels, killed the boys tending to them, and ran off. I barely escaped to bring you this awful news."

Thought was impossible. Movement was impossible. I do not know what Job was thinking. Like me, he was without words. And then it happened, that which could never be, that which was too insufferable to survive. I knew it when I saw the wild-eyed approach of the servant who had escorted our youngest daughters to the home of Primus. I knew even before he was able to gather his breath and form the words.

"A tornado came out of the desert and struck the house of Primus, pulling the walls of the house down on your family. Dead. They are all dead. All dead."

He came apart in uncontrolled sobbing. I think the other servants just looked on in horrified silence. I am not sure. Everything blurred and clouded over. Job fell up out of his seat, staggered up to the altar, tearing his clothes off as he went, and fell face down in the ashes. The altar had lost all color. The whole world and the heavens had turned to sickly green ashen death.

I watched myself leave my body moaning and writhing on the ground. There I left all feeling behind as I called for Timon.

"Quickly gather all the linens you can find that can be used for burial. Take my clothes; take whatever I have woven, whatever anyone else can find. Here, I am ripping these loose sleeves from my tunic. Take them. They are symbols of a dead life. Choose a couple of the household servants to accompany you to the home of Primus and begin burying the dead. We cannot leave their bodies to decay without respectful care. I will send for more help for you."

Servius and Sophronia were already near me, speechless, ashen, and trembling. Timon embraced Sophronia quickly and hurried off.

"Servius, go to Ruel. Tell him what has happened and ask him to send word to Uncle Eliphaz. I am sure Ruel will want to go help Timon bury the family. Maybe my mother-in-law will be strong enough to travel here to give comfort."

"Sophronia, there is no time to cry. Go first to my family, and tell them what has happened. They will come to help. Then go to Adah and let her know I need her comfort."

Then I turned to Zosimus and Tacitus. "Do what you can to refresh yourselves, take what you need for supplies, and go in search of any stray animals who might have escaped."

They staggered off, and I joined my body writhing on the ground.

My precious children. My Primus—your birth as fresh as if it happened yesterday. My first daughter—your sweet mouth on my breasts. My two youngest—here with us only yesterday. Dear Nefer, delivered with such love into Job's hands. All my children—so loved, loving, respectful, and blessed with good health. All our dear servants—gone. Job—so handsome, strong, pious, and respected. Job, I need to be with you.

I think I did not have the strength to walk. I guess I crawled to join Job in the ashes. Poor Job, his whole purpose focused on worshiping and praising God. Was it less than an hour ago that we were thanking God for all his blessings? Was it less than an hour ago that we believed God was fair and just? I lay next to my husband as well as I could, but my agony kept me writhing in pain and anger.

"Job, Job, my dear Job. How could your God do this to us? This is so unfair."

I was too shocked and exhausted to stand, yet I could not stay still.

"Job, my dear Job. I cannot bear to see you unclothed. Let me send for someone to find a robe for you. Job …"

I had no desire to touch him, nor did he reach out to me. There was no way either of us would be comforted.

As I faded in and out of the world, I ached at the sight of my Job naked. With each lucid moment, I begged him to allow me to find coverings for him, but he made no response, and I had no will to raise myself from the ashes and act without his desiring it. The day darkened and turned again to light before I felt enough to know my anger.

"Job, how could your God do this to you?" Job's answer came from the depths of his despair, like an animal's empty, tortured groan, "Dara, I was born naked; I will die naked. What the Lord has given, he has taken away. Blessed be his name."

With whatever feeble energy I could dig out of myself, I was angry at his acceptance and at his god. And Uncle Ruel had sold me the idea that Job's god was just!

My heart ached to see Job's suffering. I had lost everything, but he had lost his god's favor, the one thing that had ruled his life for so long now. I had lost everything, and he had lost more. I lay with him throughout the day, but we could give each other no comfort.

Townspeople had begun to gather, mostly to stare in curiosity and to mock. How eagerly some people take joy in the fall of a great man. Young people especially gathered to ridicule his nakedness as he lay in the ashes. Job begged for all to leave him alone. No one could fully understand or share his grief, not even I. He wanted to be alone with his god, I think.

No matter how deep my own grief, I could not suffer watching Job in his agony. I raised myself from the ashes and sent for a couple of the household servants who survived and told them to erect a tent around him where he lay. At least he would be protected from the cruel laughter. He did also agree to clothe himself in sackcloth.

The servants were clearly uncomfortable being around him. It reminded me a little bit of the trouble Sophronia and Timon had sitting with the rest of us at Adah's. A breakdown in the space between master and servant can be unspeakably painful, even humiliating. The servants felt the mortification of the fall of their leader more than they could stand to watch.

The effect pervaded the entire city. After all, most had built their faith on the justice and fairness of Job's god. Certainly what had happened was not fair. Some of them began to worry that they would also be mistreated by Job's god just as he had been. I think Astarte was removed from hiding in a number of homes. Indeed, I had thought to return to Astarte, wondering whether these disasters were her punishment for abandoning her.

Others did not lose their faith in the justice of Job's god, but instead began to search for ways in which Job deserved this disaster. Many, whatever they were thinking and feeling, brought food to our servants to provide for us, along with offers to make a gift of one of their animals. Only a few spoke to us directly, and then with eyes averted and mouths tremblingly distorted. All were speechless and impotent as they tried to grapple with the truth of our family's destruction.

The personal cloud of thick, gray woe which engulfed my emptiness sucked off whatever strength I might have had as I struggled to breathe. I thought the comfort of loved ones around me would restore me, but days passed before anyone was able to arrive. In the meantime, the focus of whatever life I had left was entirely on Job, who refused to eat. I understood that. I had no desire for food either, but I forced myself to take water and milk and some flat bread. I joined him frequently where he had raised himself to a sitting position in the ashes inside his tent, begging him to accept the bread and cheese I brought to him, but he refused.

In the midst of attending to Job, or struggling to take in air, I was assaulted by images of my children—sometimes laughing, sometimes crying, sometimes just being present, and sometimes lying distorted in death—sights that I shut away immediately, only to have them pierce through the fog again. The smiling images were just as painful as the death scenes. I became more and more distraught, frantically seeking to do something. I knew not what. There was no dirt floor of a tent to sweep; carding wool helped only for a few minutes; there was no one to tell my anguish to. I found the basket with my doll and Astarte. I tried holding each of them in turn. There was no comfort there.

Eventually, helpers did begin to arrive. I had lost all sense of time, but at some point, many of my sisters and brothers came with their families and gifts of food. Several of them had gone out first to see whether they could help to round up some animals who might have escaped the raiders and the lightning. They had little success, but, as they pointed out, the way of sheep and goats is that a few will, in time, become many. Zosimus and Tacitus returned with similar news, and with the same hope that those they had found would multiply. They were exhausted but, I think, relieved that they had been able to do something helpful, and ready to refresh themselves with food and a long rest. I knew also that they would now allow themselves the time to relive the horror and to mourn. It was important to leave them alone.

With the arrival of my family, I felt I was reaping some of the results of my own actions when I had temporarily overcome my own shock and grief to dispatch the servants. I was overwhelmingly grateful to them. I even realized that I might possibly feel gratitude to God for whatever good tidings came our way, though that gratitude was certainly tempered by the injustice of what had happened.

I longed especially intensely for the return of Timon. Some unreal part of me hoped this had all been a bad dream, and I imagined Timon might come back with a smile on his face. One look at him when he returned, and I knew I could no longer deny the reality that I would never see any of my children again. Now I ached to hear details of their death and burial. How and where had he found them? How did they look? In what linens or other weavings had he buried them? Had Ruel's family arrived to help? Poor Timon; what a terrible task. He had been nauseous when he found them, and almost fell ill again in telling me. But he did give me the details, awful as they were. He seemed to understand that I needed to know them. I nursed the information over and over again and shared it with Job, who listened speechlessly. I knew that Timon would never be the same again after this experience. He knew it too.

And yes, Uncle Ruel had been there to help. Poor Uncle Ruel. What terrible grief. He arrived a few days later, having returned home to fetch my mother-in-law. We all sat in silent support. No words would help. I thought being together would ease the grief, but it did not. Nothing could relieve the agony except for total numbness. I surged back and forth between excruciating pain and alarming emptiness.

Tragedy sometimes brings surprises. One was a visit from Jarna. She arrived alone and embraced me silently for a long time. I was strangely comforted. For a long time, we spoke no words, until she told me, "I had to come to you in your time of troubles. You were such a help to me in mine."

I hardly heard anything else she had to say. Just her presence was a gift. Later, I was able to remember her telling me that she had indeed had a comfortable life, as my mother predicted, and had given birth to many healthy children who were devoted to her. She even described what my mother had called a "potage love" that developed for her husband. I was not able to absorb the meaning of her message then, but later, I could remember that sometimes good can come out of the most terrible horror. It had for Jarna.

I waited now only for the arrival of Sophronia with Adah. I could see that Timon also was painfully anxious to see his wife. She did arrive some time after his return, with my mother and father, whose journey had been hard, as they had both developed some pain in their bodies. But Adah was not with them.

"Adah fell to her knees in tears, but she refused to come."

I made Sophronia repeat it.

"Adah refused to come."

I had thought I was beginning to regain some strength, but my insides collapsed when I heard this news.

"Why? Did you explain to her what had happened—how I needed her?"

"Mistress Dara, I begged her. She just said she could not come."

And she did not come. I never saw her again until the end of our lives approached.

I did, however, have the unexpected blessing of Jarna's visit, and I was now surrounded by family and tribe. I had community again, the kind I had thrived on in my growing-up years. Nothing could relieve my agony, but it was shared with others.

Days and then weeks passed, and Job's sadness grew deeper, his remoteness more complete. His flesh was growing yellow, hanging loose on his body. His muscles sagged. He was eating his own flesh from inside. As the days passed, he was more accepting of my sitting with him, only, I think, because he remained unaware of anything going on around him.

To tell the truth, I was beginning to get a little annoyed. I did not have the strength to have one of my outbursts, but I was erupting internally. I needed Job to be with me in our shared suffering.

If I can force myself to eat, why can he not? After all, I have lost all my beloved children. Nothing could be worse than that. And I am the one who gave birth to them. Does he think he is the only one suffering? I cannot stand to see Job like this. My friend and my strength is putrefying before my eyes.

But I did not give up.

"You must eat. You are decaying inside, and the smell of your putrid breath is terrible." Still he was obstinate, refusing to eat or drink. I told myself it was that same tenaciousness that sustained him in his refusal to give up on his god, even though he had been treated so unfairly. Indeed, it was his firm belief in the power of his god that kept him alive even as he suffered such despair. It was my own unyielding concern for Job, I think, and maybe even anger, that kept me from falling further into lonely desolation.

When he developed terrible boils all over his body, from head to toe, I redoubled my effort to get him to eat, and even to bathe. Clearly starvation and ashes were ending his life. My life was ending too. What little hope I had managed to recapture when my family arrived was spent. As time went by, Job just sat there scratching his boils with broken pieces of pottery. It was intolerable. Can you understand that I had nothing left? Even my love for Job was fruitless and unreturned, causing me only unbearable pain in my shared feeling with him. Nothing could relieve the anguish.

More and more, I repeated to myself something my mother had said long ago.

"You will see. Eventually his happiness will be yours and his pain will be yours. An attack on his body will be an attack on yours, and whenever he is spared, you will be spared. And he will know you in the same way."

"His happiness will be yours and his pain will be yours. An attack on his body will be an attack on yours, and whenever he is spared, you will be spared. And he will know you in the same way."

It became clearer and clearer. The only resolution was to die. But I could die only with Job. And he was in no condition even to consider the possibility. It seemed to me he had gone beyond the point where he was even thinking.

Finally, in my hopelessness, I knew what I had to do for the sake of both of us. Daily, I had been joining him in the ashes, for the most part, wordlessly. This time, though, I tore my own clothes into rags and covered myself from head to toe with the burnt ruins of his previous offerings to his god. This day I broke the silence.

"How long will you go on with this uprightness? Why won't you admit that your god has abused you for no just reason? Curse your god and die."

Then so will I, and this pain will end.

Job stared at me with light and life in his eyes that I had not seen since the day the trials began. The husband who had looked at me with such fiery urgency so many years ago boiled up from the depths of his soul as I evoked and challenged the very source of his power. He seemed to come alive with dismay and disbelief, and I began to tremble in awful anticipation. Fear crawled through me as I watched him straining to overcome his lethargy in an effort to make sense of my words, and the fact that I had said them. Eventually, he spoke with a clarity I had not heard from him since he collapsed into the ashes.

"Dara, I would have expected better from you. Now you are sounding like any ordinary foolish woman. We had no trouble accepting good fortune from God. Only a short time ago we were thanking Him for that. Surely now we can accept the bad fortune too."

I felt myself growing smaller and withering as I dissolved into tears—I think it was terrible guilt and awful disappointment. But there was hope there too. Job had come back to life, if ever so briefly. His look embraced me as he watched my tears. It was so much like the look he gave me when I rode off with Sophronia and Timon and Servius so many years ago in my search for peace after he challenged me to give up Astarte.

So, we would not die. My tears subsided. Strangely, I felt relieved. Though Job had clearly chastised me and, even worse, was disappointed in me, I felt his closeness and love again. Maybe it was seeing his energy. Maybe it was that old feeling of the power of his faith. Maybe it was being caught short in my own selfishness. For whatever reason, I felt better and a lot closer to Job. His eyes followed me as I walked away from him, a little taller than I had been when I joined him in rags and ashes. I kept his eyes with me throughout the rest of the day.

Job, refusing to return to the house, remained inconsolable. The only movement he made was to emerge by day from the tent I had ordered raised for him. At night, he would return to lie in the ashes. Even Uncle Ruel was politely rejected. Just as Job had torn off his clothes, I had torn away any inner consolation with which I might have clothed myself. I could not help my Job, whose body was decaying as if he were in his grave.

I remembered with awful sadness the look of love, infused with fiery power and determination, that I had sensed in him when he told me to get rid of Astarte, and briefly again when he chastised me in the pile of ashes. I would give the house and servants who remained just to see that look again, to suffer that terrible argument, even to feel the pain of my frantic search for Job's god.

His god had been the center of Job's life, and, as the patriarch of the family, his almost total responsibility. Just as I had offered the maintenance of our daily lives and wealth as a gift to him, so he had given our family and me the blessing of sacred wealth. No one could have been more pious. Once he had dedicated himself to his one god, he had never questioned his choice, never doubted his god's power, never strayed from his belief. No one's life had been so righteous, and no one was angrier than I as I watched the suffering he was enduring. The center of his life had betrayed him. There was no possibility that I could even begin to fill that emptiness. I was beginning to fear that Job's god did not even exist, at least not that god of justice Uncle Ruel had talked about. I think maybe Uncle Ruel was beginning to doubt too.

Chapter Twelve: The Comforters

Then came hope. As I was returning from another of my futile efforts to get Job to take food, I felt him stirring behind me. His body had straightened as his eyes fixed on something in the distance. It was Uncle Eliphaz approaching with his friends Bildad and Zophar. As they approached, a path opened up in which the trees and flowers emerged in their full colors. Their camels reflected gold and silver, heightened by the red, yellow, blue, and orange of their coverings. Surely now Job's salvation was at hand.

This visit by his powerful equals will comfort him. They will help to restore Job's knowledge that he is still an important and valued leader. Those jeering observers attacked him when he was weakened in every way, but now Eliphaz and the others will revive Job's sense of his own power. The agony of our losses will not vanish, but Job will at least be restored to justified confidence in himself. Thanks be to God for their arrival.

As they came nearer, they were clearly horrified at the sight of Job, and they began tearing their own clothes in a display of sympathy and grief. I wasn't sure that would help the restoration of Job's belief in his own worth, but it was a powerful demonstration of their respect.

Job was even willing to taste a bit of wine by dipping his finger, and he ate a small crumb of food when I served our guests. It was a ritual display of hospitality to his guests but did not, unfortunately, presage an increase in his ability to take sustenance. He did accept the presence of his exalted guests, and, I thought, took some comfort from their visit as they sat wordlessly with him for a week.

I had a couple of our servants erect a tent near Job's for a retreat for them at night and provide some bedding, as they refused the hospitality of the house. I was so grateful, even a bit energized myself by the process of providing them with food and drink. Their visit did not, however, have the immediate effect for which I had hoped.

Even as those wise elders sat with Job, some of our family members began to return to their own lives. I understood that, terrible as our fate was, they had their own responsibilities to tend to. Uncle Ruel and my mother-in-law remained, however, as did my parents. Poor Ruel; I watched him becoming more bent, wizened, and gray as the days wore on, even as my mother-in-law seemed to grow smaller and smaller. Job and I had lost all our children to sudden death, but maybe it was even worse for Ruel and Beta to witness this slow decay of their once handsome and powerful son.

Oh, what hope I maintained, though, in the presence of Eliphaz and his friends! What vain hope it was! After those seven days, Job finally spoke at length. What I overheard gave me no relief from my despair. While he had rebuffed my ill-advised suggestion that he might curse his god so we could both die, he clearly did not want to live. He began a long lament cursing the day he had been born. I certainly understood the feeling. I, too, wished I had never been through any of the agony. If we had never had the family and the status and the wealth and the faith, we would never have lost it.

On the other hand, a part of me rejoiced that my Job had found his voice. That terrible despairing silence was ended as he lamented, as if he were coming back to life even as he wished he had never been given life. And when he demanded that God reveal his purpose in chastising him so cruelly, I could not help but feel the strength of his faith. I may have doubted the existence of God, and maybe I was right that Uncle Ruel was beginning to lose his faith too, but Job certainly had not lost his conviction. There he was, basically demanding that God give him an explanation. You do not demand answers from a non-existent God. As for me, I longed for an answer for both of us. If anyone could help answer Job's question, it would be Uncle Eliphaz.

What I heard from Eliphaz, however, was not a comforting answer but, I thought, the cruelest attack of all. Telling him to stop complaining and accept his punishment, he accused my husband of wickedness. Eliphaz, the wise elder who had helped Job to find his way to God, who had helped him to his righteous life, was accusing him of depraved sinfulness. Job, so very pious and righteous, to be accused of wickedness. It was unthinkable. I longed for the energy to plant myself in front of Eliphaz and thrash him with words.

It did not help my anger much, but I do believe Eliphaz was trying to be helpful. Apparently, it seemed obvious to him that God protects the righteous and punishes the sinful. Is that not what Uncle Ruel had taught me? Job's god was a god of justice. Therefore, it made sense to Eliphaz that Job must have broken God's commandments in some terrible way to bring such awful chastisement upon himself. Job, he advised, should accept that God's discipline was meant to strengthen him, if only he would acknowledge his wickedness. Then he could accept the manifold gifts God would grant him in return. Eliphaz was annoyingly satisfied with himself that he had found the way out for Job. I tried, with no success, to understand that poor Eliphaz was going through an agony of his own, believing in Job's innocence and yet convinced that God punishes only the wicked.

I was dismayed by this god we had adopted. He was not the god of fairness that Uncle Ruel had sold me on. I knew that, because I knew Job. It seemed to me that there was no hope for me in any deity. Astarte no longer had any power, and Job's god had betrayed him. I was desolate.

I was buoyed with pride, though, when Job responded. No, he was not perfect. No one is. God understands that His creatures are flawed and forgives those imperfections. But as for his having been wicked, Job refused to admit to that lie. And he was not going to accept that God was always fair by human standards. Look at all the times that very wicked people live wonderful, long, wealth-filled lives. God was not as simple as Eliphaz was making him out to be.

But Job's response just served to provoke several rounds of accusations of his wickedness, with Zophar and Bildad joining Eliphaz in ever more edgy efforts to beat Job into submission. In between, Job was becoming a bit sarcastic, thanking them for being so kind in their efforts to comfort him. I could not blame him. They just would not let up. Those seven days of silent sympathy had deteriorated into what seemed to me like stubborn inflexibility as they declared themselves to be the arbiters of God's will.

Now, even when Job bewailed his condition, they accused him of ranting. They seemed to have no more willingness to comfort him in his despair. At one point, Bildad even suggested our children might have sinned wickedly, bringing about this punishment. As I listened, that was probably the most hurtful assault of all, having just lost our entire family, and knowing how Job sacrificed regularly for the sake of his children.

Somewhere in the midst of their attack on Job, I noticed that the three had once again attired themselves in their regal robes of purple. What an insult to my husband, still mourning in near nudity. So superior were they apparently feeling that I suspected they would have abandoned their tents near Job to abide in our home. I did not make the offer.

All three men were increasingly inflexible in their speeches. I tried to believe that they had Job's welfare at heart, but I confess it seemed to me that what mattered most to them now was the need to prove their own righteousness, at least to themselves. Though Job begged him to do so, Eliphaz even refused to look him in the eye to see his innocence. I had the feeling that if I were receiving the look in Job's eye, it would be a lot like the one of fiery power and determination he had given me in our argument about keeping Astarte.

Good for you, Job, I silently cheered him on.

He was suffering terribly, but he was unyielding in his integrity. The same resolution that had helped us make our way through our arguments was now strengthening my husband. He would not yield when he knew he was right. But he was not claiming to be perfect, either, not like those three "wise" elders who seemed unable, the more they talked, to see any imperfection in themselves or their convictions. From my point of view, it seemed like my Job was the only one including God in the conversation.

Job begged God to forgive whatever he had done wrong, but he refused to call himself wicked. What I especially liked was when he told Eliphaz, Bildad, and Zophar, "What sin God sees in me is between me and my God. It is not up to you to accuse me. You are taking too much on yourselves to think you can talk for God, because we cannot always understand His ways. I for one will not presume to understand them all. He is, after all, the All-Powerful. And I will not yield to your demands that I confess a wickedness that is not mine."

As this exchange was becoming more impassioned, I realized I was feeling more alive. So, I believe, was Job. What else can one do under such constant attack? I thought maybe he felt the way I did when he told me I had to give up Astarte, caught between his own integrity and the pressure to please his advisors by confessing wickedness. If nothing else, that kind of conflict creates emotion, and it is hard to remain dead when emotion has been evoked.

Personally, I was most annoyed with that youngster Elihu, who had joined the "consolers" halfway through their stay. I really did not mind too much when he sat there in silence, listening to his elders. I could hardly contain my anger, however, when he piped in toward the end of all this, as if he somehow had more wisdom, or at least more power of persuasion, to add his bit to the pressure on Job. This felt particularly insulting to me. At least the other three men were Job's equals. By this time, I was pretty tired of the endless debate. I longed for some kind of action. I suppose I even hoped that Job would call for food and wine. Anything to put an end to what I saw as this obviously fruitless debate. Little did I know how my desires would be fulfilled.

Every once in a while, Job, in his desperation, had called on God to come to him and explain what justified this terrible punishment. Each time he did that, I could see Uncle Ruel wince. I remembered what he had told me about God not wanting to be seen, so I suppose he feared that this boldness on Job's part would bring down more chastisement. As for me, I could not imagine what worse could happen. Maybe I was not a very good follower of God, but I did appreciate my husband's audacity. There were not many with my Job's courage.

It seemed right to me that Job should eventually take his case directly to God. After one last painful round of argumentative pressure to confess to what he knew to be untrue, he felt free to recite to God the whole history of his life, its long period of goodness, generosity, faithfulness, hospitality, and success, as well as the details of his suffering since the trials. Then, as if speaking to a judge in a court of law, he challenged God:

> "Grant me one thing only,
> and I will not hide from your face:
> do not numb me with fear
> or flood my heart with your terror.
> Accuse me—I will respond;
> Or let me speak, and answer me.
> What crime have I committed?
> How have I sinned against you?
> Why do you hide your face as if I were your enemy?"[2]

Now I began to tremble as if the entire world were quaking. What if God decided to kill Job? He certainly had the power. I was terrified I might lose my husband—my last hope, really. And Eliphaz and his friends looked pretty frightened too. Even Elihu the tag-along.

As I shook, so did the heavens. The center of a terrible whirlwind came directly toward us. The pressure on my body nearly crushed me, alternating with the feeling of being pulled out of myself. The sand stung and blinded us, even as it ripped away at our clothing and tore away at whatever skin was exposed. I knelt close to Uncle Ruel just to avoid being thrown about like a piece of linen, even as the deep green darkness enveloped us. Now I knew we would all die. Job's challenge had provoked God to destroy us all.

But that is not what happened. Instead, a Voice spoke from the whirlwind. No, a Voice *roared* from the whirlwind. All of us who heard it fell to the ground, thrust by some other-worldly force.

Chapter Thirteen: The Voices

From my position of trembling obeisance, I heard two voices in vigorous and strong-willed conversation. Dominating the exchange was the Voice of the whirlwind. I believe it was the voice of God. Job was standing now, awe-stricken but powerful in his responses. How could he be anything else? God had deigned to respond to him. What greater honor could a devout man receive?

As I heard it, the Voice was challenging Job to explain what power he thought was his that he could require God to state his charges against him as if it were any ordinary human court of law. How dare he serve God with such a legal claim? Obviously, Job had no doubt that it was God who had the power to bring these terrible events about, or he would not have called on Him as he did. I think the Voice recognized that. In my dread, I remembered when Job told me it was okay to be angry with God, because it showed the depth of my faith.

In the end, though, the Voice never explained to Job why he had tormented him. But there is no way I can describe the power of what the Voice did say. It was a long, thundering speech in which God (I still believe that is Who it was) first demanded of Job whether he would challenge His righteousness. Did Job think his justice was superior to God's? Could Job create and control the world as God could do? Did Job believe he could dictate justice to God? The Voice created a beautiful, wild, and often violent picture of the world over which he had dominion. Creatures great and small, good and evil, were formed by Him. Mostly, he asked Job questions. Wisely, Job gave no answer. How could he? Maybe he could not speak even if he wanted to. His hand was over his mouth in a gesture of awestricken silence.

As the Voice spoke, I found myself thinking of all the gods I used to believe in. This Voice seemed to encompass the combined authority of all those deities. Never before or since had I experienced such dreadful command—all in this one Voice. I cannot imagine that any human being had ever felt such power. Job did not yield his stance, though. He did admit to the Voice that he had spoken of things he didn't understand. Who would? No human being could even imagine creating and exercising such dominion. There was no doubt this was the All-Powerful contending with Job.

I will not go on trying to describe this event. It would be total futility for me—for anyone—to attempt to convey the awesome majesty of that Voice. I can say, though, that God never did answer Job's charge, and Job never did yield his integrity. We all knew, however, that we would never again pretend to understand God's justice, and Job humbly admitted as much to his God. Nor would we ever again doubt that we had been visited by God the All-Powerful.

Never would any of us who were there with Job forget the trembling invasion of God's power into our total beings, a gift, as I saw it, beyond all imagination. And never would any of us forget God's graciousness in what He did before He left us. I suppose it was pretty selfish of me, but I was so proud of my husband when the Voice declared that Job had spoken the truth. I think he was referring to the fact that Job had admitted a few times in his discussions with his companions that evil was not always punished and good was not always rewarded. Maybe God also appreciated Job's unyielding honesty. Or maybe that is just what I especially admired.

Be that as it may, God chastised Eliphaz, Bildad, Zophar, and even Elihu for speaking what was untrue. I think God was referring to their stubborn insistence that good deeds were always rewarded in this world and evil was always punished, as if they could dictate to God what his justice should be. God left no doubt that only He has control over good and evil.

His parting chastisement to Job's erstwhile comforters was the demand that they provide Job with new wealth from their own herds. His parting grace to Job was the promise of even greater wealth than we had enjoyed before, and a new family equal in number to the one we had lost. Maybe it was God's way of admitting that He had been unfair in His treatment of Job. Maybe that is just a human idea that I have imposed on it. Whatever the case, the blessing was profound.

And then God left us without ever leaving us. I was transfigured as if by a lightning strike that filled me with divine energy which, nonetheless, allowed me to live—no, beyond living. I had never known such transformation. If I could have seen myself, I think I would have observed a glowing aura. I did see that in the others. Uncle Ruel was standing tall. Eliphaz, Bildad, and Zophar were rooted in place. My mother-in-law had regained her height. Even Elihu was changed.

But all I cared about was my Job. The Voice had invested him with the power to stand and confront Him, but when the air softened, turning a pale orange-yellow again, and the heat rose in calm waves around us, Job fell to the ground, too weak to stand. It was he who ordered Timon and Servius to help him to our room in the house. Nearly carrying him, and very gently given the lack of flesh on his body and the terrible boils on his flesh, they lay him almost reverently on a new bed. I ran ahead to cover it with the very soft linen undergarment I had worn on our wedding day. Tucked away in a special place, it had escaped the gathering of burial cloths on the day of the disasters. Now it would serve to ease the pain of lying on the boils which seemed to be the only thing that covered the bones of his starved body.

Removing all coverings from his body to ease the pain of touch, I slowly bathed and oiled his body, in much the same way that I would many years later prepare it for burial. He did take some beer and a bit of flat bread, but he had been so long without nourishment that his desire for food would increase only very slowly. For both of us, the exhilaration of the awesome encounter with God stood in sharp contrast to the awful desolation and grief of our loss. I fear that my unceasing tears sometimes stung his open sores as I tended to him. But I was no longer alone in my grief and joy. My Job was alive with me again.

Job knew that his parents would want reassurance that he was well, so he asked me to cover him briefly so they could pay him a visit. For Uncle Ruel and Aunt Beta, the contrast was for them, as for us, awful in the mutual presence of elation and devastating grief. Because he was too weak to do it himself, Job asked his father to sacrifice the fatted calf that had been set aside to celebrate our children's reunion. The subsequent feast should be shared with our entire town.

And so there was rejoicing—subdued rejoicing, but rejoicing nonetheless. Their leader had been restored and even elevated to kingship. Our families experienced the muted celebration as well, many returning to praise God for his goodness.

The body takes time to heal, but weeks of eating, drinking, bathing, and strengthening eventually restored Job to the fully healthy, handsome man he had been before the trials began. Moreover, victory now shone throughout his body as he stood tall in the awesome awareness that God had presented himself to him.

This was a new Job, blessed with a power beyond any he had known before. Uncle Eliphaz and his companions knew it. There was no doubt that Job had been crowned king by their God, and king he would be. A just and gracious king who would never presume to know more than his God. I wanted to assume that Uncle Eliphaz and his group had been equally transformed, so that they would never again be as self-righteous as they had been.

As for me, I could never doubt again. I had heard the Voice of God. I had received a blessing like no other, thanks to the unyielding faith of my husband. I knew I would never cease to mourn the family I had lost, or lose my love for them, but strangely, my grief was infused with the God-given discernment that death is the great equalizer that we can all count on achieving. Was not that what Job had been saying when he bemoaned the fact that he had been born in the first place?

Our children had enriched the world with their lives, and they had died, as we all would. As Job had said, "What the Lord has given, he has taken away; blessed be his name."

Now I understood. What gifts we had enjoyed in the past; what gifts God had bestowed upon us now; what gifts he promised us for the future! They were gifts, not wages for our good works. I had no doubt that Job and I would use those gifts for goodness and justice.

I knew as well, beyond any doubt, that my grief would always lay heavy on my body. Understanding and discerning can help, but the loss of all one's children changes life forever.

Chapter Fourteen: After the Rejoicing

After the feasting on the sacrificial calf came the full awareness of all that had transpired. Job and I were left alone with the few servants who had survived. It took Timon a long time to recover his vigorous self. Sophronia seemed at first not to know what she should do to provide aid and comfort to any of us. I can understand that. I hardly knew what to do myself. Tentativeness prevailed in all our interactions. We were, in a sense, babies starting over again to establish a new way of life. Only Servius seemed to be his old solid, mostly expressionless self. The awesome joy of God's visit was muted by a pall of grief.

Job and I never again sat where we had been when the news of the trials was delivered to us. Just being there raised the horrendous emotions of shock and dismay. While I felt a new strength and pride, I never did lose the sense of a huge, empty cavern inside me where my family had been. Often, I would see my dear children in my dreams, only to awaken to the emptiness of their absence. While I felt the continuing power of God's presence, I had a bit of trouble sensing His nurturing love.

I appreciated the gifts He had bestowed upon us after appearing in the whirlwind, but I could not forgive Him for subjecting us to such horrible pain. He had promised us another family equal in size, but in His omniscience, He must have known that you cannot replace a child with another. I guess perhaps I should have felt guilt for judging God in that way, but I comforted myself with Job's reminder that only if we have a real faith in God can we let Him know our angry thoughts. And I did have a deep faith in God. How could I not, after hearing and sensing Him in the whirlwind?

Between Job and me, a new and different love developed—something beyond a "potage love." Only two people who have suffered such pain together can, I believe, experience the depth of connection and commitment we enjoyed from then to the end of our lives.

With restored health and strength came a new pleasure in sexual love—not so exciting as in our first marriage (yes, it was as if we were married anew), but deeper and, somehow, more spiritual. Out of that love came the first pregnancy of our new family. Truly, I was not as joyful as I had been before Primus's birth. I had thought I was done with birthing, and now I was starting over. Each change in my body, each sensation of a heavy internal rock, each cramping of my legs, reminded me of my sweet lost children. It was hard not to think of this little one as an inadequate replacement. At the same time, I feared for the future of this baby as I had never done in my previous pregnancies.

The time for the birthing came a little over a year after our trials. Outwardly, it was much the same as for the arrival of our firstborn. My mother was there supporting my back, and my mother-in-law was present to receive this child. Several of my sisters were there, as they had been before, to ease the pain and help with a swift delivery. And, as the pain seized my abdomen, they were all ready to encourage me to push. I did. I delivered the firstborn of our second family. But then, the most dreadful happening occurred. Shrieking out of my lungs, from the very belly that had just released our new daughter, came a hemorrhage of amassed pain, a surge of tears, a volcano of blackness, the river of tearful groans never sufficiently spent for my first family, the scream for Primus and all who followed.

Job, breaking the taboo against entering the women's quarters, rushed in, anticipating a scene of violent death. Indeed, death had visited along with the afterbirth.

Dear God, you cannot take our children without knowing that the mourning will never end.

I was totally lost in my own personal whirlwind of grief. I realized afterward how torn Job had been between containing my wild emotions with a restraining, comforting embrace, and providing for our beautiful new child the gentle holding she deserved. Sharing my wild anguish, he held my arms close to my sides in firm, controlled, mutual agony.

Sophronia was present to clean and swaddle our baby, while Job calmed me sufficiently to see our newborn for the first time. Once I was spent and lying on the bed that had been prepared, Job turned to our new daughter.

"She is beautiful, Dar', calm and peaceful like a dove. Her name is to be Jemimah (Dove). This firstborn of our second family is not a son, but she shall receive all the inheritance rights of a male child. That shall be true of all the daughters we may have, for God has shown me the equal value of the feminine, as have you."

He held her gently, even as he had coddled Nefer so many years before. Then he placed her to my breast, and love for her surged from me even as the early fluid flowed from my breast in reaction to her determined, birdlike, dovelike sucking.

This child was not a replacement for our lost children. She was a wonderful little person in her own right. Our love for her was as deep as that for our other children had been, but with a special overtone of awe and fear of this delicate life entrusted to our hands.

There was no dramatic announcement of her birth to a crowd waiting for the news, but a relieved and happy spreading of the word throughout our new household and, indeed, our whole city. In all, I birthed a new family of ten children. Two sets of twins helped to build our new family more quickly. True to his word,

Job bestowed on our two other daughters names that conveyed their beauty; the second daughter was Keziah (Cinnamon), and the third Heren-happuch (Eye-Shadow). Each received Job's blessing of equal inheritance with our sons. His devotion toward them reminded me of the special place I had enjoyed with my father so many years before, and even of the special affection I had always received from Uncle Ruel.

Job and I took pleasure in a long and blessed new life together, enjoying more wealth and power than we had experienced before. I want to be clear, however. Our love, though new in many ways, also retained the quality of the old. Neither one of us had given up our stubbornness, though I would prefer now to call it persistence. However we name it, my mother's prediction held. We did have our arguments, and we did refuse to give up on each other and our convictions until we had arrived at a resolution.

I never did lose the perpetual ache for the lost children of our first family. Indeed, each new birthing was accompanied by mourning for the children of our past. Job and I rarely spoke of our mutual grief, but it was always there, mixed with the potage love, and even with occasional figs and pomegranates and special cheeses.

Sophronia, Timon, Servius, and all the other servants who had survived the trials eventually recovered energy and spirit, sustaining them through long and fruitful lives. Never forgetting that we are all created in the image of God, we all recognized that we each had a different function in the living of our daily lives, but that our value was equal. Each of them enjoyed in some measure the palatial development of his city that accompanied Job's elevation to king.

In time, each of our parents departed quietly in blessed, comfortable death, as did Uncle Eliphaz at a great old age. And so, in the end, did my husband. Quietly, with his family by his side, Job fell into the permanent sleep. I think his last words were, "What the Lord has given, he is taking away; blessed be his name."

Or maybe those were my thoughts.

And so I sit here now, in the great hall of the king, mourning the end of my story, for Job is my story. I wish I could say I have such faith in God that I am not sad. But I cannot. The depth of my grief is different from the agony I felt at the time of the trials, but somehow more bottomless. Job's death is my death too.

My reminiscences are done. Once again, I am aware that Adah is here in the great hall with me. I have not fallen on my knees with her, but pulled her up to meet my daughter Jemimah.

"This is my dearest and oldest friend," I am saying through my tears. "This is Adah."

My life has come full circle. Adah is trying to tell me why she did not come to me during the time of trial. But she does not have to. I know.

"And then," she is saying, "I could not come later, because I had not come then."

I know.

"Adah, I am so grateful that you are here now. I am the one who should be asking your forgiveness. I failed to understand how burdensome my demands on our friendship were for you as the differences in our wealth grew. I know now. My gifts and visits felt like condescension and my invitations like a summons. But Adah, our friendship was only sleeping for a while. You have restored it."

Adah and I are both widows, with devoted families in whom to take pride. I want Adah to come live with me, but I understand that she cannot. She has, however, raised a tent with some of her family on the outskirts of the city. I expect once again to experience the familiarity and comfort of her home. Job is gone. My life is returning to the source.

Addendum: The Story of the Story

The issue of forgiveness seized my attention in the mid-1980s, at a time when I was still engaged in the psychology of women, my special area of instruction during the last fifteen years of my academic career. An essential aspect of forgiveness is concern for justice. Given that I also have a lay student's interest in the Bible, it probably isn't surprising that I chose to study biblical justice as reflected in the Book of Job. And it seemed especially appropriate to view the story from the point of view of his wife, who suffered the severe losses of the trials along with him. So my interests coalesced in what seemed to me to be a very comfortable and meaningful way.

Applying my psychologist's focus to the study, I found myself annoyed with the somewhat pervasive portrayal of "the patience of Job" as a kind of wimpy, uncomplaining acceptance of any punishment, no matter how unjust. I saw him instead as a pretty strong character, one of the first Self-actualizers who knew his own strengths and weaknesses and would not yield to anyone's pressure to lie about himself in order to gain favor. I liked that Job.

My career as an academic had schooled me to examine everything I could about a topic of interest. That isn't bad training if one is working on topics that are already familiar and if the amount of relevant material is reasonably limited. So I began reading about the Book of Job and discovering interesting interpretations and speculations. But when I visited the Yale Divinity School Library and saw the huge wall of writings about Job, I realized I'd either have to give up the project or curb my perfectionism. I wasn't a theologian, and previous researchers had been more abundant than I could handle and still maintain my own life and professional activities.

I confess that the dilemma froze my Joban activities, but he was never far out of my thoughts. Then, in 1992, Safire identified Job as "the first dissident,"[3] not that different from my Self-actualizing Job, I thought, and I was fired up again. The perfectionism yielded a little, and I thought maybe I could continue to explore Job for pleasure, not as if I were writing a dissertation.

The Job I liked had a firm commitment to justice rather than self-righteous justification. In 2000, my sister provided me with a book by Alan Dershowitz[4] which helped me understand more clearly the covenant relationship which Job invoked in his demand that God declare the charges he had against him. Like a good lawyer, Job called on his right to know, and the demand was justified with God's appearance to him and the ultimate restoration of his family and wealth. And I felt a little more free to enjoy Job.

Not only was Job a Self-actualizing dissident with the courage unyieldingly to maintain his integrity, he was also an early feminist. Why else would such a point be made that he named the three daughters in his second family and saw to it that they got an equal share of the inheritance? To name is to grant power, as is inclusion in one's will, so to speak. Of course, the biblical story doesn't mention the daughters in his first family. He probably named them too, as he would have done all his children. But the writer of Job chose to make a point of his care for the three daughters in his second family. Something must have happened during the trials or as their consequence to inspire him to act in such a counter-cultural manner. So Job himself opened up the issue of the women in Job's life.

Job's wife is mentioned three times in the Book of Job (New Revised Standard Version [NRSV]). First, in 2:9–10:

> "Then his wife said to him, 'Do you still persist in your integrity? Curse God, and die.' But he said to her, 'You speak as any foolish woman would speak. Shall we receive the good at the hand of God, and not receive the bad?' In all this Job did not sin with his lips."

The most common understanding of this encounter has been, over the centuries, to accuse Mrs. Job of being in league with the devil. That interpretation is a little unsatisfactory, since neither she nor Job knew the exchange that was taking place between God and The Satan, or the Accusing Angel,[5] who, by the way, was then an agent of God and not the devil we have come to know in later times.[6]

Other explanations include the suggestions that the word for "curse" could also be translated "bless," that Mrs. Job is invoking a customary Jewish usage of the opposite to express the real meaning of her intent, or, in a more humorous vein, cartoons and poems about the nuisance Job is, sitting around in the ashes, while she has to do all the work. ("Lift your legs," she says to the seated Job in one cartoon, while she vacuums under his feet.)

Those of us who study the history and psychology of women are not surprised by the identification of Job's wife with the devil. It has been tradition, until feminist reexamination changed our way of looking at things, to identify women with evil. But that's another fascinating and ongoing study of women in the Bible, which can wait for another time.

I have chosen to extract three major points from this encounter, the first of which requires knowing the situation from outside, when God tells The Satan to spare Job's life. In my story, I have chosen to see that Mrs. Job's life was therefore spared since, as Job's wife, she was one with him, a part of him, and therefore covered by the injunction to spare his life.

If you see that as a stretch, I understand why, but two other points seem more obvious to me, and, I think, may be more acceptable to you. His reply to her, essentially saying, "Now you sound like any foolish woman" suggests to me that he holds her in high respect, surprised when she sounds foolish. Like the claim in the previous paragraph, I have chosen to make this respect an integral part of the story of Mrs. Job.

Finally, this exchange has provided the opportunity for a clear statement from Job that God is in charge and may mete out both good and bad. There is nothing in this response that would reflect the views we will hear from his so-called comforters, who are so convinced that punishment is always justified and must reflect sin on the part of the sufferer. Therefore, they "know" that Job can end his suffering if only he will tell God he's sorry he's been such a sinner. The position of the "comforters" is that people can control God by their own right behavior. Job's position puts God in charge. Theirs puts humans in charge. By the end of the story, God confirms Job's argument that humans do not have the power of self-justification and rebukes the other men for their self-aggrandizement.

And now, for the second time, Job's wife is mentioned: "My breath is repulsive to my wife" (19:17 NRSV). That his breath is repulsive is no surprise. Ill and depressed, Job has not been eating, a natural consequence of which is halitosis. But I think there's more to be gleaned from this about their relationship. Clearly, she has been close enough to him to be offended by his breath, so we know he hasn't driven her away, literally or figuratively. And I also read into this an intimacy strong enough that she can come right out and tell him his breath is bad. I choose to see that kind of intimacy as an integral part of their relationship.

Finally, "If my heart has been enticed by a woman, and I have lain in wait at my neighbor's door, then let my wife grind for another, and let other men kneel over her. For that would be a heinous crime; that would be a criminal offense; for that would be a fire consuming down to Abaddon, and it would burn to the root all my harvest" (31: 9–12 NRSV).

If one really wanted to, one could find explanations—probably legalistic—of other meaning behind these words. But for me, it seems most simple and direct to accept this at face value—that he has been faithful to his wife. True, in the society of Job's time, he might have taken other wives or concubines, but it seems to me like a stretch to go beyond this simple statement of monogamy. I have chosen for my story to assume that Job and his wife respect and love each other.

Working since 1970 with secular textbooks and articles about women, I encountered an occasional reference to Proverbs 31:10–31, "Ode to a Capable Wife" (see Appendix). It has often been presented as a negative example of how hard a woman's life is. Women sometimes recognized it when I incorporated it into my talks, but Jewish women's groups always nod in positive reaction to "the woman of valor."

As I thought about the women in my own extended family, I realized how many of my aunts fit the picture of this woman, who is basically in charge of everything involved in daily life: buying, selling, merchandizing, traveling, dispensing charity, sharing wisdom, providing the necessities of food and warmth. And, unless they are living in dire poverty, these are the women who feel good about themselves, productive, useful, and respected. Depression was more likely to develop for women who were assigned a more dependent role in our culture.

I came to understand that the ideal wife in Proverbs 31 had an important function and freed her husband to perform his, which was, at that time, to study, worship, and sacrifice to God. While the culture of the 1970s valued buying, selling, merchandizing, traveling, dispensing charity, sharing wisdom, and providing the necessities of food and warmth as primarily an honorable masculine function, to really understand women of the time of

Proverbs 31, we had to understand the different culture. If Job, in standing respectfully before God, was an honorable Self-actualizer, then so was his wife as she went about her busy, productive life of tending to daily needs.

Now I knew I wanted to write the story of Job's wife, and I felt comfortable with the psychology of it. But this is a biblical story, so I needed some confirmation from an appropriate scholar. I called Brevard Childs, the noted Old Testament scholar at Yale,[7] and asked him if it would be appropriate to take the ideal wife of Proverbs 31 as a model for Mrs. Job. His answer was an unhesitating yes. The Book of Job and the "ideal wife" are both part of wisdom literature, probably from the patriarchal period. And he encouraged me to write it. Little could either one of us know how long it would be before Mrs. Job finally got birthed.

Professor Childs is not responsible for any of the other assumptions I've made in writing this story. He is, however, responsible for my developing the courage to write it. As I understand it, wisdom literature is exactly that—attempts to define and teach wisdom. It was for that reason that I chose to name Mrs. Job "Dara" (Wisdom). Equally in the running for a name was "Hope," which, I felt, reflected a particularly strong element of her personality, but perhaps hope is just one small part of wisdom, so Dara she is.

The book of Mrs. Job is fiction, but there are two areas where it has to be faithful to the source. First, while the interpretation of the particular events of the trials and their aftermath are mine, their depiction must be true to the biblical story. Second, the details of their life must reflect the reality of the time in which they lived.

My sister, the one in the family with the MFA in writing, has told me that one reads, takes notes on, and experiences a lot of material, but when it comes to writing fiction, all that serves as background against which the story is created. She finally helped free me of my academic perfectionist trap. Her final nudge was to give me a very attractive journal to be used only for writing about

Mrs. Job. What follows is some of the background that informed Mrs. Job's story as I was freed to create it.

Essentially, in my research, I have found no scholar who claims that the Book of Job is the description of a particular man, his friends and family, and the events of his life, though there may be those who believe in the literal inerrancy of the Bible who will disagree with me. I hope that they too can enjoy whatever wisdom there is in my story of Mrs. Job. I have found scholars, however, who have made suggestions about Job's location in time and place, and some have suggested men of history who may have been models for the character Job. Since no one is really sure about Job's roots, what follows is a description of the choices I've made.

The Book of Job is part of wisdom literature, which includes Job, Proverbs, and Ecclesiastes in the Hebrew Bible. There is no definitive agreement on who wrote the Book of Job, or even how many authors were involved, but a good guess is that the poet/author was writing somewhere between the ninth and sixth centuries BCE and may have placed the story as far back as 2200 BCE. There is general agreement that the Job of the story was an Edomite, or alternatively, from Uz, which is in the region of Edom. I have chosen to identify the Job of my story as an Edomite, because it gives me context for many aspects of my story.

The Edomites were semi-nomads who followed their herds in spring, summer, and autumn and lived within a walled city in the winter. A characteristic of Edom as revealed by a search of the Internet is that at least some of their city homes were in caves. Edom was located on the eastern side of what we call the Dead Sea, largely in an area which is now part of Jordan.

Choosing to identify Job as an Edomite helped define many other parts of Mrs. Job's story. Edom is another name for Esau, whose mother and younger twin brother, Jacob, basically cheated him of his father's blessing and the heritage that should have been his (Genesis 27:1–40). When Jacob fled to his Uncle Laban to escape Esau's wrath, Esau took as an additional wife the daughter of Ishmael, the son of Abraham by Hagar the Egyptian, Sarah's slave girl. He did that knowing it would offend his mother.

Choosing to accept the Edomite background for Job, then, opened up the possibility of understanding Job's piety as that of one converted to a lost faith—lost because of the heritage of anger and resentment. In the background of my thought, I see Eliphaz and the others, along with Job, recovering the God of Abraham and his sons Isaac, patriarch of the Jews, and Ishmael, patriarch of the Islamic faith.

Every bit as important in the story of Esau and Jacob as background for Job is the reconciliation that occurred, basically because of Esau's forgiveness, when Jacob returned with his family and flocks to the land of his father. As he approached Edom, the land in which Esau had settled, Esau met him with an embrace (Genesis 33: 1–17). Without the fact of that forgiveness and reconciliation, it would have been harder to portray the generosity and ultimate piety of Job.

The background for my assumptions about Job's heritage was aided even further by another exploration of the Internet, where I came upon an article on the site http://www.nabataea.net/, "The Hyksos, Kings of Egypt and the land of Edom: Chapter IV: The Book of Job" (most recently reviewed 8/17/07).[8] Here, I found the suggestion that Job is modeled on King Jobab, who, if I understand the site correctly, can trace his lineage back to Esau. Please understand that I am in no position to claim or dispute the accuracy of these assumptions, but they do allow me to embed my story in a reasonable framework. Here is the lineage: Esau fathered Ruel and Eliphaz (and King Bela?). Ruel fathered Zerah, who fathered Jobab. In adopting this base for my story, I am, therefore, making Job the great-grandson of Esau and a relative to Eliphaz.

But here's the wrinkle created by artistic preference, or something like that. I had almost finished the first draft when I realized that, to be true to this assumption, Job's father should have been Zerah, not Ruel, as I had been calling him. So, I set my computer to work changing all the "Ruels" to "Zerah." Uncle Ruel was gone from my manuscript, and instead, there was this stranger, Uncle Zerah. Now I know what writers mean when they talk about identifying with their characters. I actually went into mourning over the loss of Uncle Ruel, whom I had come to love, and I perceived Uncle Zerah as an undesirable intruder. After a conference with my writer sister, I concluded with her help that, since this is fiction, I could bring Uncle Ruel back—a great relief to me. Then Pastor Beth Warpmaeker, much to my delight, pointed out that Zerah would have been Ben Ruel (son of Ruel), so I can feel even more justified calling him Uncle Ruel for short.

Now you have a pretty detailed description of the choices I have made on the way to creating "The Book of Mrs. Job." I love Job and Dara. I also enjoy the issues of justice, self-justification, grace, and the masculinity/femininity of the deity. I am a psychologist, and it's mostly the psychological questions that drew me.

I have come to love the other characters in the book as well. Since they are largely my own creation, I guess that's a way of loving myself. So be it. They say that writers don't really create anything new, that they write about what they have experienced. Looking back at the story, I guess that says something either about my own positive experiences in life, my own optimism, or my own Pollyanna tendencies. Whatever the reason, I see that I haven't created even one mean and nasty person, except perhaps for the nameless attackers who brought on the trials.

I have also been pleased by the comment of Pastor Dave Olson of Mount Calvary Lutheran Church. He pointed out what the Hebrew tradition sees as the purpose of biblical stories. It is to promote discussion in-depth of the issues raised. I guess that's what Job was doing as he worshiped God, and I like to think that's what I am doing in seeing the story of Job in this particular way.

Mona Gustafson Affinito, Ph.D.

Please remember, I'm a psychologist, a therapist, maybe a writer, but not a theologian or a historian. I've just tried to get Mrs. Job's story right.

Appendix: Proverbs 31:10–31, "Ode to a Capable Wife"

A capable wife who can find?
She is far more precious than jewels.
The heart of her husband trusts in her,
And he will have no lack of gain.
She does him good, and not harm,
all the days of her life.
She seeks wool and flax,
and works with willing hands.
She is like the ships of the merchant,
she brings her food from far away.
She rises while it is still night
and provides food for her household
and tasks for her servant girls.
She considers a field and buys it;
with the fruit of her hands she plants a vineyard.
She girds herself with strength,
and makes her arms strong.
She perceives that her merchandise is profitable.
her lamp does not go out at night.
She puts her hands to the distaff,
and her hands hold the spindle.

She opens her hand to the poor,
and reaches out her hands to the needy.
She is not afraid for her household when it snows,
for all her household are clothed in crimson.
She makes herself coverings,
her clothing is fine linen and purple.
Her husband is known in the city gates,
taking his seat among the elders of the land.
She makes linen garments and sells them;
she supplies the merchant with sashes.
Strength and dignity are her clothing,
and she laughs at the time to come.
She opens her mouth with wisdom,
and the teaching of kindness is on her tongue.
She looks well to the ways of her household,
and does not eat the bread of idleness.
Her children rise up and call her happy;
her husband too, and he praises her.
"Many women have done excellently,
but you surpass them all."
Charm is deceitful, and beauty is vain,
but a woman who fears the Lord is to be praised.
Give her a share in the fruit of her hands,
and let her works praise her in the city gates.

(NRSV)

Endnotes

1 Jemimah is the name given to Job's oldest daughter in the biblical story.

2. Mitchell, Stephen. The Book of Job. San Francisco: North Point Press, 1987, p. 35.

3. Safire, William. The First Dissident: The Book of Job in Today's Politics. New York: Random House, 1992.

4. Dershowitz, Alan M. The Genesis of Justice: Ten Stories of Biblical Injustice that Led to the Ten Commandments as Modern Law. New York: Warner Books, 2000.

5. Safire, Op. Cit., p. 3.

 "In many translations, the definite article precedes the word Satan in the Old Testament, suggesting a title like Special Prosecutor, or Inspector General, rather than a person's name."

6. Pagels, Elaine. *The Origin of Satan*. New York: Random House, 1995, p. 39.

 "In the Hebrew Bible, as in mainstream Judaism to this day, Satan never appears as Western Christendom has come to know him, as the leader of an 'evil empire,' an army of hostile spirits who make war on God and human kind alike. As he first appears in the Hebrew Bible, Satan is not necessarily evil, much less opposed to God. On the contrary, he appears in the book of Numbers and in Job as one of God's obedient servants—a messenger, or *angel* …

In biblical sources, the Hebrew term the *satan* describes an adversarial role. It is not the name of a particular character."

7. Taylor, Barbara Brown. "Who are the Bad Guys?" *Christian Century.* May 3, 2003: 43.

"Minus one cryptic reference in 1 Chronicles, Satan first appears in the Book of Job, where he works as God's prosecuting attorney. Satan cannot do anything to Job that God will not let him do. When Job's children are killed, they are killed with God's permission. When sores erupt on Job's body, they erupt with God's permission. As hard as this is for Job or his readers to swallow, it is one of the occupational hazards of monotheism. There is "only one God in this story—the God who forms light and creates darkness, according to Isaiah 45—the God who makes weal and creates woe."

8. I have been saddened to learn of Dr. Child's death in the summer of 2007.

9. http://www.nabataea.net/, Gibson, David J. "The Hyksos, Kings of Egypt and the land of Edom: Chapter IV: The Book of Job" (most recently reviewed 8/17/07).

About the Author

Mona Gustafson Affinito, Ph.D., emeritus professor of psychology at Southern Connecticut State University, emeritus faculty at the Adler Graduate School in Minnesota, psychologist in private practice in Chaska, Minnesota, mother and grandmother, has published several books on the psychology of forgiveness. www.forgivenessoptions.com

Printed in the United States
137943LV00003B/9/P